BOOK 3 – SUMMER

BEAUTIFUL DEAD

Eden Maguire

Hodder
Children's
Books

A division of Hachette Children's Books

Typeset in Berkeley Book by Avon DataSet Ltd,
Bidford on Avon, Warwickshire

Printed and bound in Great Britain by
CPI Bookmarque Ltd, Croydon, Surrey

The paper and board used in this paperback by Hodder Children's Books
are natural recyclable products made from wood grown in
sustainable forests. The manufacturing processes conform to the
environmental regulations of the country of origin.

Hodder Children's Books
a division of Hachette Children's Books
338 Euston Road, London NW1 3BH
An Hachette UK company
www.hachette.co.uk

For my two beautiful daughters

WOODMILL HIGH SCHOOL

Who decides what's normal and what's not?

People around here sigh and say, 'No one died in six months, thank God. Maybe the worst is over.'

I say, 'Wait, it's not finished, not by a long way.'

'No one else died. Now we can get our lives back on track.'

'Ride the bus into school, why don't you? Go to work, don't dwell on the past.'

Fine, I think, but I keep my cynical mouth shut and put one foot in front of another along with the rest of Ellerton.

Normal is grey and narrow, normal is not daring to look back.

At night I dream in widescreen, high definition technicolour.

Phoenix is there, centre screen, full of life. He's coming right at me, smiling, reaching out his hand. I take it and his blue-grey eyes shining out from under a sweep of dark hair are

1

talking to me, telling me he loves me. When he rests his arm around my shoulder, I feel the warm weight of it.

Awake, I'm alone. They try to get near me – Laura, Zoey, Logan and the rest. 'Look ahead, Darina. There's so much to live for.' Meaning, you're seventeen years old, for chrissake, you only knew Phoenix Rohr for a couple of months. OK, so you lost him in a street fight and that was tough but you have your whole life in front of you. Normal, grey stuff. I push them away. I prefer my multicolour dreams.

Phoenix and me cross-legged on a rock in the middle of Deer Creek. Silver flashes on the clear water, blood-red sun over Amos Peak.

Phoenix's lips on mine, full and soft. I run my fingers from the nape of his neck down his spine. His skin is smooth, warm and tanned, there's no angel-wing death mark between his shoulder blades where the knife went in. It's like we've been together since the day we were born.

Awake again, I'm driving out of town. I'm cold, it's March and the grey voices are winning.

'I fixed up more sessions with Kim Reiss,' Laura, my mom, just informed me. 'Please talk to her, Darina. It's bad for you to bottle up your emotions this way.'

I'm cold, pushing eighty miles per hour with the top down. The way the wind flaps through my hair reminds me of beating wings. The mountains ahead look black.

What do I say to Kim the shrink in her primrose-yellow room? I'm cold, I'm hurting, I haven't seen my Beautiful Dead boyfriend in four whole months. Sixteen weeks of driving out to Foxton since Arizona stepped into Hartmann Lake, her angel wings spread wide. It was late fall, before bleak Christmas and a blank New Year. I stood next to you, Phoenix, at the lake's edge, while angel-winged Arizona walked up to her waist in the clear green water and a mist came to take her. 'Go,' we said. You held my hand and your hand was cold as ice.

Foxton is where I'll find you and it won't be a dream. One cold day in the deep snow, when your overlord decides it's time, you'll be there at the barn door, waiting for me. Maybe today.

Black rocks rise sheer to either side, a grey strip of road threading through. The car engine whines and the wind tears at me.

Today. I picture Phoenix at the barn door, back from the dead, here on the far side. The frozen chambers of my heart fire up. I'm in his arms and this time I will never let go.

1

For once I did something Laura asked me to do – I went to see Kim Reiss.

'Do you think I'm crazy?' I sit in her yellow room and the words spill out of my mouth. 'Or is this normal?'

I'm still driving out to Foxton on a daily basis and still the place is empty. I'm searching for ghosts. We're almost through March; the snow is melting.

'Tell me how you feel,' Kim suggests. She's reading my face, picking up my body language.

'Broken.' That's the best word I can come up with, here in this calm space. *I won't cry.* The second I think this, I have to reach for the Kleenex. How come I have so little control over my tear ducts?

'Explain "broken" to me.'

'Not working. Minus my hard drive.'

Kim studies me. 'Are you eating? Are you sleeping?'

I shrug.

'That's a no. Are you going into school?'

Ellerton High, where there are four empty desks, one each for Jonas, Arizona, Summer and Phoenix. And everyone acts like those kids never died.

'Yeah.'

'I take that as another no. Which bits are not working, Darina?'

'My head. I don't see things. I don't listen. I forget everything. That can't be normal, can it?'

'What else?'

'Here.' I strike my chest. *Come on, heart, wake up. Remember to beat.* 'I don't feel anything. I don't know how to act.'

She hands me another tissue. 'Is there one thing in particular that preys on your mind?'

Phoenix, where are you? When will you come back and haunt me? I don't care if you're real or if I imagined the whole deal. Just don't leave me here alone!

I body swerve. 'It's almost a year since Summer died,' I tell Kim.

'Summer Madison – one of the four teenaged victims. Was she something special to you?'

'To me. To everyone who knew her. I can't explain.'

'I read in the newspaper that she was a musician.'

'She played guitar. But it was her voice. You never heard anything like that voice.'

'They say she was ready to sign a record deal.'

I nod. 'It's weird – you can go on YouTube and listen to her sing, as if she's still here.'

'But she'll never walk into a room and say "hi" again. Is that it?'

I'm staring at the small, neat scar on Kim's left cheek. I don't want to go where she's just taken me, I'm wondering, *How come the scar?*

She sits alert in her soft cream seat.

'Did I tell you I was there?' I ask.

'Where?'

'In the mall, the day Summer died. I was drinking coffee in Starbucks. She was coming out of the music store. She saw me and waved, started to walk towards me. Then the gunman opened fire.'

She never made it.

Summer Madison – everyone knows her name. She has a million hits on YouTube; there's a video of her on stage at a festival when she was fifteen years old.

'Hey, Darina,' she would have said if she'd reached Starbucks. 'I just printed out some sheet music for a new song. Do you want to come over to my place and hear it?'

We would've driven out of town to Westra to her house stuffed with guitars and keyboards, her mother's artwork spilling out of the studio: the smell of wet oil paint; her dad cooking up a storm for their evening meal: the aroma of onions, tomatoes and basil. She would've sat me down on the terrace overlooking the mountains and picked up her guitar. She would've sung like an angel.

But no. Instead, Psycho Man showed up and sprayed the mall with bullets. I watched Summer go down mid-stride at the foot of the escalator and waited where I was until the shooting stopped. Maybe thirty seconds. When I got to her she was lying face up and blood was oozing over the white marble floor.

'Darina, I'm leaving for work.' Laura appeared at my door and winced when she saw I was logged on to Summer's angelvoice website. Hannah Stoltman plus Parker Simons and Ezra Powell, a couple of techies from Ellerton High, set it up soon after Summer was killed, in her memory and with Summer's parents' blessing. Kids use it to review Summer's tracks: *These songs are five star! So sad she died – I couldn't stop crying!*

'I said I have to go now.' Laura wanted me to be out there meeting my friends, getting over it, normal and grey. 'Will you be OK?'

'Yeah, I'm cool.'

'Jim has the day at home to catch up on desk work. Ask him if you need anything.'

'OK, cool.' *Why in a million years would I do that?*

'Will you go to school?'

'Yeah.'

'Good. How did the session with Kim Reiss go?'

'Good.' Did I mention my back was turned? *Tap-tap-tap*. I faked interest in my keyboard.

'And will you go again?'

'Next Friday, April first.' *All Fools' Day.*

Laura nodded and left. Five minutes later I was in my car, heading for Foxton Ridge.

There was snow on the ground and flakes falling gently from a dull grey sky. I parked by the stand of aspens and stood near to the iron water tower staring down at the big empty barn and the ranch house dwarfed beside it. Snow turns things new and bright – except for the fact that there were no footprints or tyre marks in the yard you would've sworn the place was inhabited.

Do the Beautiful Dead have footprints? I wondered. They don't have heartbeats or blood running through their veins, so it was a reasonable question. I looked up at the sky and felt cold flakes settle on my face then melt.

I would walk down the hill, I would pull open the barn door and look inside. The door would creak. A creature – maybe a mouse or a squirrel – would scuttle up the wooden stairs into the hayloft.

This had happened many times. I was always moving clumsily, weighed down by despair. *Phoenix isn't here. Phoenix isn't here.* Hammer blows, doom and gloom.

My feet crunched in the snow. I passed the razor-wire fence, mended last year by Jonas and Hunter, and slowly approached the rusted truck parked in the yard. It was old and broken down. It would never move again. Catching sight of my reflection in the windscreen, I glanced quickly away. Whose was that skinny, ghostly image wearing mascara and cropped, dark hair, its face pinched with cold? Not mine. I didn't recognize the scowling, downturned mouth, the dead eyes. I looked again. *Hey, Darina, that is totally you!*

Turning my back, I made for the barn door with its crazy pattern of hammered nails, its zig-zag of support planks, the grey, weathered boards. Looking up, I saw the dead moose head staring down at me with giant antlers and glass eyes.

Creak! The opening door scared the crap out of me.

Come on, Phoenix, where are you? There in a corner beside the rakes and shovels, reaching up to tear down a

10

century of cobwebs and stepping forward? Standing on the wooden steps to the loft in a narrow ray of light, flecks of dust doing a dizzy dance around your head? *Smile down at me, for chrissake. Reach out to me and take me by the hand.*

It was weird but I kind of liked Kim's room. The aspen trees outside the window were pale and bare, but inside there were cosy chairs and a coffee table, a warm rug and a calm, scarred face waiting for me to begin.

'Thirty seconds,' Kim said. 'Between the shot that hit Summer and you reaching her.'

'A lifetime,' I told her. I liked the way my therapist had styled her fair hair – shorter than usual, showing her small ears and dangling blue earrings, kind of ethnic but classier . . . moonstones maybe. 'I shouldn't have waited, should've been there sooner.'

'And risked getting shot?'

'Yeah.' They said Summer died instantly, so logically it wouldn't have made any difference. Her eyes were open but she wasn't seeing anything. I leaned over and spoke to her. 'I told her I was sorry.' Did I get through? They say that hearing is the last sense to depart.

Kim waited to see if I needed to lean forward and grab a tissue.

'No way were we alike,' I explained. 'Summer has

this long, blonde hair way past her shoulders. She's real delicate.'

'But you two clicked?'

'Always.'

'She sounds amazing.'

'She is.'

'Is?'

'Was,' I said.

'You're not the only one who misses her.'

Whenever Hannah was around, she made sure I couldn't wallow. She'd called at my place with Jordan and Logan the day after the April Fools' session with my therapist. It was Saturday and they'd decided I needed to get up off my ass.

'We all miss Summer.' Jordan made it clear. 'That's why we did the Christmas concert and why we plan to do another one for her anniversary.'

'Don't bale out again,' Hannah warned. The three of them were sitting on my bed while I stood by the window blocking the light. Hannah was growing her blonde hair long and Summer-style; I don't know if she knew it. Jordan was giggling and showing Logan a text on her phone, leaning in close. *Good*, I thought. *Now maybe Logan's attention will be off me*. Well, maybe there was a twinge of jealousy in there somewhere, along with the relief.

'I came to see the Christmas concert,' I argued. 'I just couldn't take the pressure of standing up there and having people watch me while I played Summer's songs.'

'Plus, there was Phoenix,' Logan reminded them. 'Darina still wasn't over him, remember.'

Mr Sympathetic. *Please concentrate on Jordan's glossy dark hair swinging across your cheek, her pop-princess perfume and her fluttering lashes.*

'OK, maybe I should cut you a little slack,' Hannah agreed. 'But face it, Darina, you need to get a life. Come down the mall, help me buy some shoes.'

I went, not because it was an offer I couldn't refuse, but because I ran out of excuses. Jordan and Logan browsed CDs in *the* music store while Hannah chose shoes. I was there but not there.

The snow had melted on the driveway up to Kim's place. Piles of the stuff were heaped to either side. Snow is ugly when it gets to this stage – the mounds look like dirty shrouds covering old corpses.

'We could work out ways of helping you move on,' Kim suggested at the start of our session. Today she was wearing stud earrings, not danglers, and a pearl necklace. I thought they made her look older.

13

My face must have been a total blank.

'Or we could pick up where we left off last time and work through what happened with Summer.'

We could, I thought, *but I don't have the answers. I don't know who killed her – that's why she's back at Foxton, one of Hunter's Beautiful Dead.*

'If I was my friends, I would've given up on me,' I told Kim out of the blue. 'Likewise Laura and Jim.'

Her eyelids flickered. 'They don't give up because they *care* about you, Darina. What do you want to do here today?'

Suddenly it was on the tip of my tongue. *Summer is not dead. And neither is Phoenix. Well, they are, but they're the living dead and I still see them. You could too if I took you to Foxton and we fought our way through the barrier they set up – the wings and other weird stuff. Except they went away after Arizona left for the last time and so far they haven't come back. They will though – Phoenix and Summer will reappear with Hunter. They have to – they're the Beautiful Dead!*

I jerked forward and gripped the arms of my chair.

'Darina?' Kim said.

Tell her! Let it all out, about how Hunter controls them and reads everyone's minds, how he brings them back here to the far side even though they died, and he protects them and sets up the barrier so that no one except me can get through, and that's only because I'm useful and because Hunter knows I'm hooked on Phoenix. I'm their link with the far side and no way am I supposed to share this with you!

Only, the secret is too big and it's breaking out here in this cream-and-yellow room, with the clock ticking on the wall and Kim standing up and edging towards me to sit me up straight after I've gone dizzy and toppled forward against the glass-and-steel coffee table.

'Drink some water,' she said, offering me a glass.

Like a robot I took it and sipped. I was dizzy, I'd lost my balance, hearing what I thought was a breeze drifting in through the window. I'd looked and seen the window was closed. The breeze grew stronger and I recognized it. Wings were beating inside the room – many, many invisible wings. It was all good news.

Kim was holding my glass steady, my heart was thumping hard against my ribs. 'Do you hear that?' I asked.

But of course she didn't. Only I could hear a thousand wings beating hard, telling me that the Beautiful Dead had come back.

Night still falls early at this time of year. It was already dark when I drove past the blue neon cross set against the steep hillside at Turkey Shoot Ridge.

15

They're back! I told myself over and over. I knew it for a fact. How else would I have heard the wings, felt them beating me back from any confession I might have made in Kim's office? Ask me how I felt when I fainted in front of her, and I'd say there was no terror, just sheer joy, because Phoenix was waiting for me at Foxton, less than an hour's drive away.

But this is weird – they're dead people and you're rushing blindly to meet them. I heard Hannah's grey voice telling me this as I drove on. *That's gross, Darina. You make my flesh creep.*

Jordan wouldn't say it to my face. She'd wear her worried expression and discuss it with Logan. He would tell her how much I'd changed, how he couldn't get close to me any more and he'd given up even trying.

The black sky was vast, speckled with faint silver stars. A mule deer startled me by leaping out of the brushwood and into my headlights, almost sending me off the road. I gripped the wheel and drove on.

At last I reached Foxton and the string of small wooden houses lining the highway. I threw a left at the old store, along the dirt track that followed the creek deeper into the mountains. I passed the spot where Matt Fortune and Bob Jonson had ridden their Harleys over the cliff.

I recalled the moment – the roar of the two engines

before they cut out, the perfect arcs they made in mid-air as they fell from sight. And then there was silence, and my certain knowledge that their deaths had freed Jonas.

My tyres squealed as I took the bend. I left the fishermen's shacks behind and headed on into emptiness. Not much further now before I reached the end of the track.

There it was – the water tower on the ridge, more visible at this time of year because the surrounding aspen trees weren't in leaf. Moonlight made the white trunks almost glow in the dark, acting as a beacon as I slammed the car door and began to run towards them.

Come on, wings, bring it on! I thought. I was expecting to run into the barrier that kept out strangers, the weird sensation that a million wings were forcing you back, sending your head into a spin, thrusting demented visions of skulls at you, hovering overhead, grinning and sightless. Hunter and the Beautiful Dead did that – they had powers to raise the dead and send you screaming down the mountain a jabbering wreck, where no one in their right mind would listen to you but they would hand you strong coffee and tell you that it wasn't real, you'd had a bad trip, and no wonder considering what had happened around Ellerton this past year – the four dead kids and all.

I reached the water tower and there was silence. There

17

was no wind, nothing to stop me from treading on through the frozen snow, down the steep slope past the fence, hearing my feet crunch through the surface, feeling myself sink at each step until I reached the empty yard.

Zoom back to the view from the ridge and how did I look? I was a small black figure surrounded by white slopes, standing knee-deep in snow. I turned towards the house, changed my mind, decided to head for the barn instead. There were no lights, no sign of movement nor any clue that people had lived in this place for decades.

Zoom back in, study my haunted face – dark eyes glittering – my trembling hand as I pulled at the barn door and it gave way. You can see that after the high of my experience in Kim Reiss's room, I've lost hope again, am in despair.

Phoenix. I try to whisper his name but nothing comes out. Nothing disturbs the silent shadows of the ancient barn.

Hunter is playing mind games. He made me believe I'd see Phoenix, just to keep me hooked. The truth is he's not ready to let the Beautiful Dead return, but he wants to keep me enslaved. Believe me – Hunter the overlord would throw me into this kind of torment without a second thought.

I stared into the blackness of the barn. I sensed, but

couldn't see, its high roof arching over my head, the broken stairs to the hayloft, the rotting wooden stalls where they once stabled the horses.

Then I went back out into the yard – a tiny black figure lost again in a gigantic white bowl. What did I do now? Walk out of the valley away from my dream.

I set off. At first I didn't look back. I'd come there on a surge of hope, like a huge wave gathering strength until it crests and breaks. I went away a spent force, to a hollow sound of pebbles sucked from the shore.

I was halfway up the hill when something made me turn. I could see the square hulk of the barn in the moonlight and the empty log cabin across the yard. Nothing had changed. I turned again and continued on my way.

'Darina.' A soft voice broke the starry silence.

I clenched my jaw, refused to turn. *No, you don't, Hunter. Not this time.* But I did stop walking. I waited and listened.

'Darina, it's me.'

'If this is another mind game . . .' I said, turning at last.

And there was a light in the house porch. It swayed and flickered as if someone was holding up an oil lamp, standing in the cold, wanting me to return.

Finally! Yes, I turned and ran, staggered, stumbled down the hill. I was sobbing out of relief, blinded by tears, blundering against the razor-wire and ripping my jacket as I fought free.

The light flickered on the porch. 'It's me,' Summer said.

You can tell a whole lot through someone's voice. It's not usually the first thing you notice, but when you pay attention you learn if they're chilled or if they're tense, happy or sad – you don't even have to look at them.

Take my own voice. I talk fast and soft. Jim is slow and loud. It makes me want to say, 'Keep the noise down, I already got the message, thanks.'

Voices match their owners. Think about it, test it out – you'll see what I mean.

Well, Summer's voice fits her, and it's special.

'It's me,' she said, holding the oil lamp above her head.

She melts my heart every time she speaks. It's like honey; it makes you think of meadow flowers swayed by a warm breeze.

I stumbled on to the porch. She led me inside the house, into the kitchen where she put the lamp on the table and waited for me to catch my breath.

'Is this for real?' I gasped.

She smiled and nodded. 'Hey, Darina. Take it easy, huh?'

I closed my eyes and opened them again. Summer was still there. 'Where's Phoenix?' I asked.

'He's on his way. He'll be here soon.'

'When?'

I looked into every corner, ran upstairs to the bedroom, came down again.

'Summer, I need to see him!'

'I hear you,' she said softly, a sigh mixed in with the words. 'I understand.'

'My God, you stayed away a whole lifetime!' I slumped in the rocking chair by the empty grate. 'I've been a wreck back here.'

'I know. But you know Hunter – he makes the rules. He said no way could we come back until he was ready.'

Taking a deep breath, in then out, I tried not to sound bitter. 'So now he's finally allowing it to happen. What changed his mind?'

'He found someone he was looking for, then came to fetch us – me, Phoenix, Iceman and Donna.'

I counted the Beautiful Dead as she named them. 'What happened to Eve and her baby?'

'I have no idea. She wasn't in the group. We know not to ask questions.'

'But don't you wonder?'

'Yes.' Summer pulled her red woollen jacket close across her chest – the collar was embroidered with small white flowers. She wore a cream woollen scarf around her neck. 'This time it's just me, Donna, Iceman and Phoenix, plus the new guy.'

'A new guy?'

'Older, like Hunter. That's all I know.'

'So how come Hunter sent you ahead of the others?' I already guessed the answer – it was Summer's turn. She stood in line to be set free, after Jonas and Arizona, before Phoenix.

'Tomorrow is my birthday. After that, I have twenty-one days before the twelve-month anniversary.'

I had her birthday written in my diary, along with the date of the shooting – Saturday, April thirtieth. It was also engraved inside my head, burned on to the inside of my eyelids, acid-etched on my retinas – in other words totally unforgettable.

'Hunter sent me to fetch you,' she explained.

'You were there with me in Kim's room?' Of course she was there, using her zombie power to stay invisible, listening to every word and setting up the winged barrier. 'It's funny – Kim thinks my problem is that I'll never see you walk into the room and say hi again.'

22

'I know,' she smiled. The shrink's mistake appealed to her sense of humour, which, like everything else about Summer, was subtle. 'You did good.'

'I was about to fall apart,' I argued. 'I could've wrecked the whole thing for you.'

'But you didn't. You haven't breathed a word.'

I sighed. 'Knowing that if I did, Hunter would never fix for you to come back to the far side – not you, or—'

'Phoenix,' she interrupted. Her face in the lamplight was indistinct, her eyes shaded. She lifted a hand to push a strand of fair hair behind her ear. 'It's tough for you.'

'Tough doesn't cover it,' I laughed. 'Think of a sword hanging over your head, ready for you to make one minuscule false move. If you do – *whoosh!* The blade goes for your jugular.'

'Ouch!' There was a silence, broken by the *pop-pop-pop* of the flame in the lamp faltering then plunging us into darkness.

'Out of fuel,' Summer explained, moving across the room towards the table where she unscrewed the top of the bowl-shaped well and poured in more paraffin. The sharp smell caught in my throat then a match flared and the lamp flickered back on. 'I want you to do something for me,' Summer said quietly.

'Anything.'

23

'Tomorrow, on my birthday, go visit my mom and dad.'

'OK.' I sounded cool with this, but didn't feel it. Summer's dad, Jon Madison, would most likely handle my visit, but her mother, Heather, was a different story. She was the high-strung artistic type and the rumour was she was nowhere near being over Summer's death.

'It's going to be tough,' Summer warned. 'I'd go myself, but Hunter says no.'

'You're not to go near your own house?'

She shook her head. 'There'd be too much emotion flying around – me seeing my mom and dad, revisiting my old home. He says I wouldn't handle it.'

'Is he right?'

'Totally,' she said with a sigh. Then, more pragmatically, she added, 'Our overlord is always right.'

'So I'll visit for you,' I promised. 'Tomorrow midday. I'll report back, no problem.'

'And between now and then you have to drive home.' Summer came close and looked me in the eye. 'That's another of Hunter's orders.'

In the split-second it took for me to take in this information, I felt my stomach knot and I clenched my fists. 'No. I need to be here when Phoenix arrives.'

'I won't fight with you. I'm only passing on what Hunter

told me: "Say hi to Darina then send her home. Tell her to wait there until I call for her."'

'Wait? I've already waited a million years. Please, Summer, don't make me leave.'

I would stay there for however long it took. I would be standing in the barn doorway when the wind rose and the invisible wings beat, there when Phoenix materialized in a halo of soft white light.

Summer was kneeling beside me, staring into my eyes. I wasn't ready for it when she zapped me with her zombie strength and destroyed my willpower. Her eyes shone cold into mine and my head was sent spinning into an alien space – I was floating and weak as a kitten, ready to do whatever I was told.

'Sorry to do that to you,' she murmured as she led me out of the house and across the yard.

I couldn't fight it, not if my life depended on it. I was out of there minus my free will, heading up the snow-covered hillside towards my car.

Summer's voice drifted in the wind after me – the soft, love-song voice of my best friend who, second to Phoenix, I missed most in the world. 'Hunter will call you back soon,' she promised. 'And I swear to you, Darina – Phoenix will be here.'

2

There was blood on my hand. I hadn't noticed how it had got there but I was in the bathroom, washing it away when Laura knocked at the door.

I watched my blood mingle with the clear water in the basin.

'Darina, are you OK?' She sounded like she was trying to stay calm, but inside she was freaking out. 'Where did you go? Do you know it's past midnight?'

'I'm OK,' I insisted. 'I was chilling, forgot the time.' I splashed cold water on my face then dried it with the towel, opened the door of the wall cabinet and reached for a Band Aid. 'Go back to bed, Mom.'

'I couldn't sleep until you came back. I was waiting for the sound of your car.'

I pictured her hovering on the other side of the door, one hand clutching her dressing gown tight around her neck. A brick in the wall I'd built between us suddenly dislodged and I got a glimpse of what I was putting my mother through. Sliding my injured hand into my jeans pocket, I opened the door. 'Da-dah! See, I'm cool.'

Laura was pale; her eyes looked darker because of the smudged mascara. She was exhausted. 'Why can't we be . . . you know . . . the way we used to be?' she pleaded.

She meant me aged ten jumping off the school bus and running up the drive, her baking cookies, me kicking off my shoes in the hallway where Dad would trip over them when he came home from work. Yeah, she baked cookies back then. I practised gymnastics out in the porch.

'We're cool, Mom.' I pushed past and disappeared into my room. *Nice try, Darina, but you're not fooling anyone.*

Jim noticed the Band Aid over breakfast. 'What happened to your hand?' he asked.

'Nothing. I cut it on a can.' I'd sat down at the kitchen table but I was only pushing cereal around my bowl, letting it go soggy. I was fixated on waiting for the call from Hunter.

'Did you sleep?'

'Yeah.'

'You don't look as if you did.'

I narrowed my eyes and stood up. I try not to say more than two words in any sentence I exchange with Jim. And a conversation never lasts longer than thirty seconds.

He saw me grab my keys from the shelf by the door. 'Where are you going?'

'Out.' Anywhere rather than stay in the house with him. Understand, the guy has done nothing bad except get together with Laura after Dad left. He isn't an axe murderer or anything.

I got in my car and drove to town. It was still too early to visit the Madisons, so instead I chose a coffee in *the* Starbucks, plugged in my iPod and sat listening to some of the tracks Summer had laid down for her demo CD. On what would have been her birthday it seemed like the appropriate thing to do. There was a sad song she wrote for Zoey after Jonas died and Zoey was going through her surgeries, not knowing if she would walk again. Summer's words about not getting to say goodbye seemed to get right inside Zoey's head, to say what she must be feeling. The song was called 'Red Sky', and the guitar was the saddest thing you ever heard.

'Hey, you.' Jordan walked up to my table with Logan in tow.

'Hey.' I took out my earpiece, steeled myself for

upbeat advice from Jordan and reproachful looks from you-know-who.

'Cool,' she told me.

'What?'

'To see you at the mall. Today especially – Summer's birthday.'

'It's no big deal,' I argued. 'Besides, Jim was driving me nuts.'

They sat opposite me, Logan's legs way too long to fit under the table so he stretched them out to one side, blocking me in.

'You don't look great,' Jordan told me.

'Thanks. I was going for pale and interesting.'

'Mission accomplished,' Logan muttered.

Jordan nudged him with her elbow. 'School sucks,' she reported, pointedly missing out any reference to my absences from recent rehearsals for Summer's concert. 'I'm late with two assignments.'

'Only two!'

She grinned, then got up to order coffee, which left me and Logan trying not to meet each other's gaze.

'It's not what you think.' Eventually he leaned across the table with his hands clasped. 'Jordan and me – we're not . . .'

'Does *she* know that?' I shot back. Jordan's body

29

language told me a whole different story.

'I told her straight – I just want to be friends.'

'Logan, for chrissake – work it out!'

'I'm not into Jordan,' he flustered.

He still didn't get it. 'It's not all about *you*.'

Anyway, what was there not to be attracted to? Jordan is tall, curvy, high-cheeked, wide-mouthed adorable. She has long, dark, wavy hair to die for.

She came back with two lattes. I picked up my iPod. 'Enjoy!' I told them as I stepped over Logan's legs and made my way past the spot where the madman had aimed and fired.

It was like waiting by the phone for the most important call of your life, only multiply that a thousand times. My mouth was dry, my heart racing as I took the elevator, found my car, then drove out of the car park.

Maybe I should've stayed inside the house. That's where Hunter expects me to wait. I almost turned for home, afraid that I'd missed the vital signal that he was ready for me to go out to Foxton.

But the promise to Summer couldn't be broken. I signalled left and headed for Westra.

Like I said, the Madisons live in a big house on the edge

of town. It's set on a hill with open views of Amos Peak to the west, but compared to some of the houses out there it doesn't make you feel like you shouldn't walk on the rugs or sit on the couches. Summer's parents aren't into glitz.

Maybe Jon Madison sees too much of that through his work, which is architect to the rich and sometimes famous. For instance, he designed the Taylors' house nearby – Arizona's parents are seriously wealthy through Allyson's work as news anchor for a networked TV station. She's a face on the screen in the corner of everyone's living room.

Or maybe it's Heather's taste that makes the Madison house so warm and welcoming. She's into rich colours and natural surfaces. The floors in the house are polished wood, there's pink granite on the kitchen worktops and hand-thrown pottery on the shelves.

I used to love going there. Today would be less of a pure pleasure thing, I knew.

Cars parked on the drive told me to expect to find both Heather and Jon at home, but when I knocked on the door there was no answer. I knocked again then listened. When I still got no answer I turned the door handle, pushed gently and stepped inside.

How weird was this. The hall still had the lived-in look

– jackets hanging on hooks, Jon Madison's briefcase perched on the back of the brown leather couch – but something was totally different. No, not some*thing*; some feeling. Yes, the atmosphere of the house had changed from the warm and welcoming I told you about to cold and empty, as if the spirit had gone out of the place. *Summer's* spirit to be exact. And you know what? There was no music playing – and that was totally not right.

'Hi!' I called. 'Is anyone home?'

The door to Heather's studio stood open so I went to investigate. I saw canvases stacked against the walls, a half-finished painting on an easel, but again no sign of life. On the worktop there should have been half-squeezed tubes of paint and rows of brushes waiting to be used, the smell of paint thinner in the air.

Backing out of the room, I went to peer into Jon's study at the big drawing board, the computer screens and the scale model of an art gallery he'd designed for a city in New Mexico.

Finally, I crossed the hall into Summer's room. Call it habit, because I sure wasn't expecting to find anyone in there.

Summer's room without Summer in it. Her shoes were there beside the bed as if she'd just kicked them off. A pair of jeans lay crumpled on the floor. On the wall above her desk was her one-year-old schedule for her school assignments. One of her guitars was propped against a chair.

I drew a deep breath and turned to leave, then I heard footsteps and my judgement stampeded off. Freaking out, I decided to hide behind the bedroom door.

Heather Madison came into the room. I caught her in profile, head raised, eyes open wide in surprised expectation. She breathed her daughter's name, her voice rising on the second syllable, as in, 'Summer, are you there?'

Then I stepped into view and the hopeful light in her eyes went out. 'Sorry, Mrs Madison . . .'

She gripped the chair, knocking Summer's guitar to the floor. A hand went up to cover her eyes.

'I didn't mean for you to find me here.'

'Heather?' It was Jon Madison's turn to enter the room with a question. He saw the two of us, quickly got over his surprise and went straight to his wife. She crumpled in his arms so that he had to hold her upright as he led her out into the hall.

'Mr Madison, I'm sorry.' *No-brainer Darina, charging in like that, bull in a china shop.* At least the comparison hit the mark – Heather reminded me of a china doll, skin like porcelain, with Summer's golden hair. And I was the bull stampeding across her dreams.

He smoothed things over, supported his wife and sat her on the leather couch. 'No problem, Darina. I guess you gave Heather a shock. She's OK now.'

Mrs Madison glanced up at me to double-check the reality of what had happened. 'Darina?' she said without the rising intonation, minus the longing that she'd injected into her daughter's name.

'It's me, Mrs Madison. I came to check if you were OK.'

'It's April ninth.' Jon dropped in an unnecessary reminder, lowered his head for a second then rallied. 'Darina, it's good to see you. We invited a few people for drinks to celebrate what would have been Summer's birthday. We're out on the terrace, catching the spring sun.'

He took his wife's hand, expecting me to follow them across the hall, through the big kitchen out on to a sun terrace, where I joined a group of maybe ten guests including Allyson and Frank Taylor, and Russell Bishop – Zoey's dad.

Allyson came straight over, glass in hand. 'Good job, Darina,' she said with a sympathetic smile. 'It can't have been easy for you to come.'

'Especially since I didn't get an invite,' I said, smiling weakly back.

'Jon did this for the parents,' she explained. 'The ones who share their loss.'

'I'll go,' I said hastily.

'No.' She caught my hand. 'Sharon Rohr is here. Come and say hi.'

Greeting Phoenix's mom wasn't what I had in mind for this visit, which was already tough enough. I'd hardly seen Sharon in the nine months since he'd died – I'd go so far as to say I'd made a point of keeping out of her way. But here she was now, a small, slight grey-haired figure glancing up from the carved wooden bench where she sat, registering my presence with a shocked, hostile look, then glazing over this expression with a forced smile.

She stood up, smoothed her skirt and made herself step towards me.

'Hi, Darina, how are you?'

'Good,' I lied. 'How's Zak?' Zak is Phoenix and Brandon's kid brother, thirteen years old and at war with the world.

'Good, thanks.' She didn't expect me to believe her either. Plus, it was clear she'd already run out of things to say. After all, I was only her dead son's girlfriend, the person who'd stolen his company and enslaved his affections in the last two months before he got stabbed.

It wasn't only that – even before it happened, Sharon Rohr had always made it plain that she didn't want to be my friend.

'Come and speak with Frank,' Allyson suggested, steering me away.

At least Frank Taylor was pleased to see me. We chatted about the progress their son Raven was making with a one-on-one teacher who came to the house, and new therapy based on creative activity to help with his autism.

'Come visit any time,' he suggested. 'The door's always open.'

I tried my hardest with the chit-chat, but the visit wasn't going well. I felt Sharon's eyes drilling through the back of my head and Jon keeping a wary watch over his fragile wife. 'I have to go,' I told the Taylors. 'Bye.'

At the bottom of the Madisons' drive, I found Brandon Rohr leaning against my/his red convertible. 'What are you doing here?' I challenged. Here was another person to mess with my already messed-up head.

'You mean, "Hey, Brandon, how's it going?"' The grin he gave me was loaded with irony. 'I say, "Cool. How's the car I gave you?" You say, "She's a beauty. I totally owe you, Brandon."'

'I'm not in the mood.' I stepped to one side as he launched himself free of the car and stood upright just centimetres away from me.

'Is my mom in there?' he asked, tilting his head towards the house. He didn't care that I was frowning and shaking my head, trying to get into the car.

'Yeah. Brandon, I need to go.' *Because you're too in my face, because you found me this car, because with his dying breath Phoenix asked you to take care of me. And because you're not him.*

'She told me to pick her up from the party.'

'She's in there, I already told you.' Now I caught sight of Brandon's black truck parked down the street with Zak sitting waiting. 'What time did she tell you?'

He glanced at his watch then up at the Madisons' front door. 'Ten minutes ago. I'm in trouble. Here she comes.'

Finally I got past him and jumped in my car. I was out of there before Sharon Rohr made it down the drive.

And now I was out of patience, through with the waiting and I was driving across town, through the Centennial district to where the highway stretched out clear into the mountains, climbing steadily with the tyres thrumming over tarmac, eating up the distance between me and Foxton.

I know – Summer said Hunter would give me the call. He'd specifically told me to wait. But she'd also used the word 'soon' and I took that to mean a couple of hours, right after daylight broke, no time even for breakfast. Not all this endless, crappy waiting, trying not to picture Phoenix coming back from wherever the Beautiful Dead stayed when they weren't on the far side, settling in with Summer and the others, maybe doing chores like lighting a fire in the house or clearing snow from the yard.

I don't do waiting patiently, never have.

So I made Foxton in record time, not bothering to stop for gas in Centennial. A weather forecast on Rocky Radio told me to expect snow before nightfall. *Just give me time to reach the ridge before the heavens open,* I prayed. The station played more Country tracks about guys in jail missing their gals, and gals getting even with their mean, cheatin' guys. I switched off the music to concentrate on frozen puddles on the dirt road by the creek.

They were only half right about the snow – clouds rolled down from the peaks but it came earlier than forecast, falling softly at first and coating the rough road with white powder. Then the wind rose and I had blizzard conditions. Snow hit the windshield too fast for the wipers to handle and pretty soon I had to stop the car to clear the screen.

Turn around, go back, a voice in my head told me. *This car isn't built to drive through deep snow. What happens if you skid off the road?*

Since when did I turn into my mom? I ignored the common-sense voice, got back into the car and drove on. But then I had to stop before I reached the ridge, after I heard the wiper motor whine and cut out. After that, it was either sit in the car with the heater running until the gas gave out, or walk the rest of the way to find Phoenix.

It was a no-brainer – I pulled out a pair of boots from the trunk, zipped up my jacket and headed across country.

Anyhow, by the time I reached the shelter of the aspens, the wind had dropped and the snow was easing. Patches of blue appeared in the sky. I told myself this was a sign that I'd done the right thing, never mind Hunter's orders, and hurried down the hill.

I was so expecting to see Phoenix, to fall into his arms and act out all the clichés. I was so convinced in my mind that I made it real.

It's clear in my head . . . He's strong as he wraps his arms around me. I'm melting at the sound of his voice, the grey world is turning bright. I feel his breath on my face.

The new fall of snow hid the hollows on the hillside, making me stumble. I didn't care that I didn't have gloves

39

or a scarf, or that packed snow wedged itself inside my boots. I was happily dreaming out the reunion.

So I was surprised there was no light on in the house, but then told myself it was still daylight. No footprints in the yard either, but the recent snow accounted for that, and like I said before – maybe the Beautiful Dead don't make marks in the snow. No smoke from the chimney. I slowed to a walk.

He's not here! It hit me like a punch to the belly so that I almost had to lean forward and hug myself to recover. *Idiot – he's not even here!*

When I thought it through it was obvious. There'd been no call from Hunter, no barrier of beating wings up on the ridge. The Beautiful Dead *always* set up the warning to keep out far-siders, even when they knew it was me. I guess that was just in case I had someone hidden in the trunk of my car – Hunter's paranoia. Anyway, there were *always* wings. I stood in the yard and wondered what to do next.

Then I remembered Summer – at least she was around, probably sitting inside the house doing that patient waiting thing that I'm so lousy at. The second it occurred to me I sprinted for the porch, but when I tried the door I found that it was locked.

Which left only the barn. That was it – Summer was

busy with chores, stacking firewood, loading it into a sack to drag fuel into the house or fixing something that had broken.

I walked to the barn door, listening out for clues. I was straining so hard that maybe I imagined it – not a sound but a presence beyond the door, a sense that the barn wasn't deserted.

I reached out my hand for the latch, then hesitated. At that moment a breath of cold wind raked through the recently fallen snow, raised a flurry of icy flakes and blew them against the door.

How cold was that wind! Sub-zero, and getting up stronger, rattling at the wide door, covering me in frosted white flakes. I had to get inside the barn or freeze to death. So I lifted the latch . . . and that was the exact moment when the perfect reunion fell apart.

They were all there – the Beautiful Dead – standing in a circle in the murky light, all facing inwards towards Hunter and a second, grey-haired guy of about the same age, who I'd never seen before. I made out Summer in the rich red woollen jacket she wore the day before, Donna in a long, grey woollen coat, Iceman in a black ski jacket, and Phoenix.

He had his back to me but he knew I was there.

'Phoenix.' I had to say his name. Surely when I spoke

he would break out of the circle and come to me.

Hunter raised his head and stared right at me. I felt the cold wind grow stronger, banging the door shut behind me.

Actually, Phoenix didn't turn. It was as though he hadn't heard, though I knew this was wrong – super-hearing is part of their thing, plus the mind-reading ability that would have told him how much I wanted to be in his arms.

Hunter was doing this to us out of spite, zombie-zapping Phoenix's willpower, keeping us apart.

'Phoenix!' I pleaded.

Hunter stepped out of the circle. He was taller, stronger than I remembered, his eyes were deeper set, his mouth a hard, thin line, and there was still the death mark on his forehead – the angel-wing tattoo where the bullet had entered his brain. He came towards me, shaking his head.

Then I don't know what happened. I saw anger in the overlord's eyes. It overpowered me and made me fall to my knees, though he didn't lay a finger on me. I was down and hurting, feeling sharp pains run through my body as my head spun and my vision went weird – like Summer's mind-zap but a hundred times stronger. Instead of Hunter's figure I saw fiery red patterns floating in the dark air, flickering to orange then fading and leaving me in a pitch-black space, unable to see. I remember reaching out for anything solid to grab hold of before the stabbing pain in my head took over and I heard the sound of beating wings fill my ears.

Waves of airy sound swept through my head, a million invisible wings, a coldness against my face. I was blind and falling. I was crying out for help but I was alone.

And then everything stopped except the echoing sound of Hunter's footsteps walking away. And then that stopped too and there was blackness.

I don't know how long I was out. When I came around, it was dark and I was alone.

I had no idea where I was or I how I got there.

I closed my eyes and opened them again. I was in a place that smelled of dust and damp. It was very cold.

After a while of lying on the floor, testing out which bits of me hurt, I raised my head and rolled on to my side, then on to my knees, where I stayed and groaned a while, arms still supporting me, my head hanging. I felt like it was filled with heavy mush.

A door blew open, then banged shut, awakening a spark of memory about where I might be. It made me haul myself upright and try to walk.

When I made it to the big wooden door, I pulled hard, met resistance, and so began to push. The door gave way and I stepped outside into the moonlight.

Did you ever have a dream where you recognize a scene – maybe somewhere where you once went on vacation but you can't quite place it, and anyway it's the wrong situation but you can't get to where you really need to be? That's the closest I can get to explaining what it was like – yes, I'd seen the old truck in the yard before, but I didn't recall where or when. Sure, I recognized the old ranch house, the porch and the log pile stacked neatly at one end, but how had I got here and why? Then I saw two guys – strangers – on the porch drinking beer. Maybe they could explain.

Ouch – my head hurt and felt weirdly hollow as I walked unsteadily towards them. The older one was facing me, the younger one wore a black ski jacket. Grey-haired, ponytail guy looked like he was angry at me. Black jacket guy must have heard me coming because he glanced over his shoulder then looked back at his companion as if waiting to be told what to do.

'Stay right where you are, Darina.' The boss man stopped me in my tracks.

I stood there shivering and hurting.

'Hunter, what did you do to her?' the younger guy asked. He was definitely worried. 'Did you wipe her memory clean?'

'And if I did?' The one called Hunter didn't blink, he

just looked at me with a stone-cold stare.

'What about Summer?' young guy asked.

He shrugged. 'If Darina doesn't follow orders, what good is she to us?'

'Does Phoenix know what you've done?'

This time Hunter's eyelids flickered shut. Released from his staring eyes, I risked another look around the snow-covered yard with a racing heart. Why were they talking about Phoenix as if he was still alive? Phoenix was dead – how loud did people have to announce it? How many times? What planet were these two guys living on?

'Phoenix is in the house with Summer,' Hunter said. 'I told Donna to take Dean up to Angel Rock and show him the territory. Dean is top of my list of priorities right now.'

'So Phoenix doesn't know you zapped Darina's mind?' The younger guy wouldn't let it drop. He even took a step down from the porch as if he planned to come and help me. Then Hunter turned one of his icy looks on him and he stopped, mid-stride.

Meanwhile I stood in the middle of this nightmare with a hole in my head where my memory used to be.

Hunter stepped down into the yard instead. My stomach lurched. I wanted to back away but my feet wouldn't move. 'What do you think, Darina – should I let you stay zapped and send you home?' he taunted. 'Maybe that would be a good idea. You wouldn't remember anything, I promise.'

I was staring right into his face, at the grey eyes shaded by the prominent forehead, the long hair swept back, the sculpted chin and harsh line of the mouth. At that moment I knew there was no arguing with him – I was totally in his power. And somehow he was the cause of what had just happened – my blackout, my hurting head, my total confusion.

'Your mind would be a blank,' he promised. 'You would be back with your family, going to school, grieving for Phoenix and learning to let go. You would put one foot in front of another like the other bereaved residents of Ellerton.'

No! I wanted to yell at him, but nothing came out. *I'll never let Phoenix go!*

'Believe me, you will.' Hunter's eyes dug deep into me and seemed to read my unspoken thoughts. 'Your connection with him will weaken. You'll continue to miss him – every day at first, then every other day, every week, until you learn to move forward and live again.'

'That's not how it works,' I said bitterly. 'You don't understand. I'll always love Phoenix.'

Hunter planned every move. He stretched his lips in a

disbelieving smile and chose that moment to let Phoenix walk through the door on to the porch. A split-second later he let my knowledge of the Beautiful Dead flood back into my head.

I fell to the ground again but this time Hunter permitted Phoenix to be there to catch me. The moment of our reunion had arrived – I was in his arms, but it wasn't how I'd imagined it; we were just puppets with the overlord pulling our strings.

Phoenix kept me from falling. He held me close and I clung to him until my head began to clear. He picked me up and carried me into the house, up the stairs to the bedroom where he laid me on the bed.

'You're going to be OK,' he promised, bending over me so that his lips were against my cheek. 'Hunter relented.'

I could see him in the lamplight and raised my hand to touch his smooth, cold skin. 'I'm sorry,' I whispered.

Phoenix sat on the edge of the bed. 'For what?' He took my hand away from his cheek and kissed my fingers.

'For angering Hunter. For messing things up.'

'Hey, Hunter upsets real easy. You didn't mean to do it.'

'Don't be nice to me! Tell me I'm an idiot for pushing his buttons.'

He smiled warily. 'You're an idiot, but you're *my* idiot.'

'You make me want to cry.' I lay with my head on the pillow, my face turned away. 'I thought I'd be so happy – here, with you again!'

'Don't cry,' he pleaded, lying down beside me. 'You're here. I'm here.'

'Where have you been, Phoenix? Why did you stay away? I know, don't tell me – Hunter is the one who makes the decisions. You don't get to choose.'

Phoenix tilted my head towards him. 'That's the deal,' he agreed. 'We have to accept it.'

'It doesn't stop me wishing that it could be the way it was before,' I whispered. With his body next to mine, his clear eyes looking at me, taking in every detail of my face, his fingers brushing my lips while I talked, I felt so close, like we'd never been apart. 'Remember how we did things back then, with no one to stand in our way?'

'I remember every second we spent together. It's stored up here.' He tapped his forehead then pressed the centre of his temples. 'You know what I wish?'

'What? That we had longer?' Two months of Beautiful Dead reunions was all we had left. Eight and a half weeks.

'That I could put it in a bottle and keep it. I don't want a moment of it to slip away, not ever. I want your voice with me wherever I am, your eyes looking at me the way they do right now, arm in arm, side by side.'

'You never told me this before.'

'I never put it into words,' he whispered. 'But you already knew.'

I nodded. 'Let the heart speak – that's what you once told me. But hearing the words is good too.'

Phoenix's smile grew warmer, got right behind his eyes and made them sparkle in the soft light. I felt myself melt as I leaned my head back and he kissed me.

'Darina, I want you to meet Dean.' Hunter introduced the new guy over the kitchen table, calling Phoenix and me down from the bedroom soon after Summer and Dean came back to the house. 'Dean, Darina is the only person from the far side who gets to know about the Beautiful Dead. We trust her with our secret.'

Was he mocking me, or was he genuine when he used the 'trust' word? I glanced at him but couldn't tell, so I switched my attention to the newcomer – a heavy-set guy with a shaved head, whose open-necked shirt showed his death mark: the dark-blue angel-wing tattoo in the angle between his neck and his collar bone.

'Dean is an ex-cop,' Hunter went on. 'A hundred punks and dope-heads wanted him dead.'

'How did it actually happen?' And why was he here?

I knew you only got to be Beautiful Dead if there was a mystery that needed clearing up. You had to deserve to come back.

'Car crash,' Dean told me. 'Severed the top of my spinal cord. Drunk driver.'

I shuddered, wondering whether or not Hunter would want me to work for Dean on the far side and exactly where he was on the list – before or after Phoenix, Donna and Iceman? All I knew for sure was that Summer was next.

'The culprit was never traced,' Hunter said. 'Dean had been following the car out by Amos Peak, ready to pull him over. The driver refused to cooperate.'

'Which is the last thing I remember.' Dean spoke like a cop – like he'd seen every bad thing a person can do and then some.

I don't know why but I felt that helping him might be harder than working for the others. Maybe it was the generation gap, or my particular problem with authority figures.

'Except that Dean radioed in the car registration plate before the crash,' Hunter added. 'Which means the details should've been on record, but evidently someone in the office got careless.'

'That piece of data was wiped from the computer, or it

never got recorded,' Dean said between gritted teeth. 'No driver was ever traced.'

'So Dean gets to come back and set the record straight.' Hunter rounded up the discussion. 'Keep it in mind, Darina. And remember, he died doing his job.'

I frowned. 'Summer is still priority, though? I mean, how many days do we have – twenty, twenty-one?' Searching for her among the quiet figures in the room, I saw her standing by the doorway and went to join her. 'I drove to your house, did you know?'

She took a deep breath. 'How was it?'

'There were people there – Allyson and Frank Taylor, some others. A party.'

'For my birthday?'

'Yeah. They were cool, though. I can honestly say that no one cried while I was there.'

'Mom?'

'She held it together, even though she didn't expect to see me.'

'Dad?'

'Cool. He's strong. I really like your dad, Summer.'

What else could I tell her? That they hadn't moved a single object in her room since she died, that her mom wasn't painting any more. I avoided the deep stuff because there was no comfort there.

She probably delved into my mind and saw it anyway.

'So now we need to focus on you, Summer.' This was Hunter speaking, and it was weird because he'd done one of his sudden shifts of tone from harsh to almost gentle. 'Tell Darina everything you remember about the DAY.' He said 'day' in upper-case letters so everyone knew what he meant. 'And Darina, please give it your full attention.'

Meaning, *tear your mind away from Phoenix, forget about yourself and your own grief for a change.* 'Why do you always think the worst of me? What did I do?' I wanted to protest, but a glance from Phoenix warned me off.

'Let's walk,' Summer suggested.

We had regular sleepovers when Summer was alive. Usually I would take my guitar to her house. We would hole up in her room, maybe play a song she'd just written, she would change a few notes or words, while I designed an album cover on Photoshop or wrote sleeve notes. We'd dreamed of her making the big time since we were ten years old.

So we were used to looking up at the night sky together, star-spotting and working out which was Orion, getting it all wrong and saying, 'Hey, there are a million stars up there. Who needs a name?'

Tonight as we walked we saw two shooting stars.

53

'So I'll find your gunman,' I promised. We were up by Angel Rock, out of sight of the barn and house. 'If that's what you want me to do.'

It was a long time before she reacted. 'Sometimes I wonder what difference it'll make to find out who did the shooting. Why not leave it at "Some crazy guy who ran away and who they never caught. End of story"?'

But we both knew we couldn't leave it hanging in the air like this. 'And other times?'

'Then I think it through and I know it makes all the difference in the world to the people I left behind.'

'Your mom and dad?

'My mom especially. She needs closure.'

We walked on a while before I asked Summer something that was bothering me. 'And you? Do you have any anger towards this guy?' The guy who sprang out of nowhere and started spraying bullets around the mall. Scrawny Psycho Man with the peak of his white cap and a pair of shades hiding his face, not even aiming before he fired.

'Anger?' she echoed with surprise.

'Why not? He stole your life. Don't you picture all the stuff you could've done – the music especially. All just gone – wiped out. Don't you hate him for that?'

'No. I think of Mom and Dad and how their lives are

on hold. That's it. That's why I'm here – to get the truth so they can move on.'

'So I guess that's me,' I confessed with a sense of shame. 'I'm angry for you.'

Summer stopped on the ridge to look at me, the wind in her hair, an infinity of stars above her head. 'All my life I wanted to be more like you, Darina.'

I stepped away and shook my head.

'Yes. The way you always know what's right and what's wrong, no grey areas. Me – I look from all angles and end up without a point of view.'

'We're different,' I agreed. 'But you're the one with the talent. We all envy you. Actually no,' I said straight away. 'No way do we feel jealous. We all want you to be this big, big star, for the whole world to know you.'

'We're talking as if it might still happen,' she pointed out, staring up at the sky.

I took her hand and stood with her for a while. Then we walked arm in arm back to the house.

The whole of the state police were still looking for Summer's killer. It was a high-profile shooting, part of the cluster of deaths that launched Ellerton into national prominence and kept it there for months on end.

'You need to dig deep,' Hunter instructed before

I left Foxton that night. 'And this time you really don't come back until you have something new to tell us – understand?'

'Got it.' My short answer came through gritted teeth. I held Phoenix's hand more tightly.

'Wait for us to come to you,' the overlord insisted. 'And be careful not to attract attention.'

'Got it,' I said again.

'So go.' Hunter turned his back and it was Phoenix who led me out of the house in silence.

'How are you doing?' he asked, halfway up the hill.

I shook my head. 'This is cruel. Why can't I come to see you?'

'Because.' His shrug conveyed the helplessness we shared. 'Hunter tightened up on the rules,' he explained. 'He doesn't want anyone following you out to Foxton – Logan or any of your buddies. You know what happens if someone from the far side finds out we're here.'

'You leave and never come back.' It was a death sentence all over again. None of the Beautiful Dead ever got another chance to unravel the mysteries surrounding them. No one got justice or peace of mind.

'So that's the risk.' Phoenix stopped as we reached the ridge where Summer and I had star-gazed earlier. 'No one's saying you got careless, Darina. Hunter's looking at the laws of probability, is all.'

'The more I drive out here, the greater the risk that someone follows me?' This discussion, which pushed me kicking and screaming back into the grey world, was making me miserable. 'Maybe Hunter should trust me more,' I pointed out. 'I'm getting pretty good at covering my tracks.'

'I know, baby.' With his arms around my waist, Phoenix pulled me close. 'I know, I know.'

'Tell me you'll still be here when I come back,' I sighed.

'I'll be here.'

'Tell me you still love me.'

This time he didn't speak. He put it all into a long, lingering kiss that told me everything I needed to know.

The next day, Sunday, I steered clear of Laura and Jim and took my laptop with me to a quiet coffee bar on the edge of town. I sat by the window, looking out on roofs and sidewalks still wet from snow melt.

'Black coffee,' I told the waitress as I logged on and typed *Ellerton killings* into the search engine. I wasn't feeling good. Maybe the coffee would help with the headache left over from the day before and the shaky, hopeless feeling of being cut off from Phoenix until I came up with some good new information on Summer.

I already knew there was a whole website devoted to recent events in town. It listed the deaths – Jonas Jonson, Arizona Taylor, Summer Madison and Phoenix Rohr, with pictures of each of the victims, together with short biographies and quotes from friends and families. The entire thing was a rubber-necker fest for people who got their kicks from sudden, untimely deaths – those onlookers who pick over details until they feel they're somehow part of the story and write stuff on the site like *Summer, I luv u so much* and *We'll miss u 4ever.* This was so not my thing. In fact, I felt queasy just accessing the site.

But where else did I start with solving the mystery of Summer's killing? I had to trawl through the tributes, the newspaper articles, police activity, autopsy report, even the reviews of her music and the links with her angelvoice website, looking for anything that jumped out.

The waitress brought coffee and looked over my shoulder at the screen. 'Are you reading about that poor kid, Summer Madison?' she asked. 'Did you hear her "Red Sky" track?'

I nodded.

'And the one about being in love with someone who doesn't know you're into them, and how that feels. What's the name of that one?'

' "Invisible." ' I didn't welcome the conversation – it was happening even though I'd turned my screen away and kept my shoulders hunched over my coffee.

'Yeah, "Invisible". So cool.' Waitress-girl was still hanging around and hoping for a reaction from me. 'Actually, I know Summer's family. My mom was their housekeeper. She says there was music and guitars everywhere. She doesn't go there now that Mrs Madison isn't doing so well. Mom says she doesn't like people poking around Summer's old stuff.'

I looked up over my shoulder. 'I'm pretty busy,' I told her.

She nodded quickly. 'Sorry. I didn't mean to—'

'You didn't. It's cool.' I waited for her to get back behind her counter then refined my search to find newspaper articles written at the time of Summer's killing. There were dozens and systematically I began to read the reports, trying to keep my own feelings at bay and not to relive the nightmare moments.

Friday, April thirtieth, four-thirty p.m. Lone gunman, random attack. Shot twice – once in the leg, once in the chest. The seventeen-year-old victim died instantly. Some facts were set in stone.

I went on to interviews with witnesses – mall employees, friends of the victim, including the comments I gave to a reporter while I was still traumatized: 'This is not happening. It can't be true.' The reporter states that I said the same short phrase over and over: 'It can't be true.' Even though the ambulance had arrived and the paramedics had taken Summer away in a body bag, and the place was swarming with cops.

Then I got into the police statements. There was the point twenty-four hours after the shooting when their investigation had thrown up a couple of unspecified leads. They were planning to interview everyone present in the mall at the time of the shooting, then a couple of days down the line they were spreading the net, appealing for any information about the missing gunman, asking the public to report anyone behaving suspiciously on the day of the shooting. Then, later still, they got into searches of abandoned cars and buildings, and as a last resort they went to Allyson Taylor's news station and recorded an appeal from Jon Madison, begging the killer to give himself up and give the family closure. Eventually, when that failed, they started to look out of state at copycat killings.

I slowed down with the mouse action to read this part thoroughly. The local newspaper stuck with the crime long after it vanished from the nationals. On June sixth they reported a shooting in Venice, Florida. The same thing – the guy walked into a mall in late afternoon, wearing a black sweatshirt and white baseball cap. He didn't aim before he fired. This time he hit three targets. Two people died, the third had serious chest injuries. And again the gunman got away. The Venice cops believed he'd parked his car close to the car-park barrier, straight out on to an intersection with five exits. He probably chose the coast road north to the Texas Panhandle, the fastest highway he could find.

I read the report twice. The white cap grabbed my attention. I got a flashback of April thirtieth – Summer exiting the music shop, waving at me and starting to walk across the plaza, a wide-open target. The face of the gunman beneath the white peak – thin and wearing aviator shades. *Why those ugly shades?* I wondered at the time, in the seconds before he pulled out his gun.

Now I sat and asked myself if the same crazy guy had driven south and chosen another mall. Had he driven from town to town until he found one with an easy escape route? Did he plan things this carefully, with chilling attention to detail?

'More coffee?' The waitress was back, snooping at my screen.

'No – thanks.' I clicked the Back key repeatedly. *Ellerton killings* came up. I was back where I'd started. This time I chose a new route and clicked on *Ellerton – a town's History of Violence.*

A journalist had written a special feature for a weekend magazine and it was reprinted here. He seemed to think there was something in the fact that a small town in the American Midwest had played host to more than the average number of killers. He claimed that the crime statistics put Ellerton in the same league as some of the major cities. 'You can't sleep safe in your beds' was his message to residents. And as a matter of fact, he told us, this curse went way back, to the start of the last century and beyond.

I read that I lived in a town that grew up around cattle – we were on the route the drovers used as they headed south from Montana into Texas, and these drovers were a lawless bunch, stealing steers from other herds, shooting each other in the back for the sake of a few dollars per head. The whole thing didn't settle down until the cattle drives dried up and Ellerton got itself a train station on the main route west through the Rockies. Then haulage companies invested and Ellerton grew respectable, on the whole.

Come the end of the nineteenth century, we had three churches and five schools. We still had cattle, but they were mainly fenced in. The ranchers' wives came into

Ellerton to shop along a main street selling hats, gloves, lace for their collars and hand-made boots.

End of history lesson, but not quite. The journalist soon got back to the gory part of our past – for example, the ancient, unsolved mystery of a rape and homicide out at Foxton Ridge. My finger twitched on the mouse button as I read on.

The name of the rape victim was Marie Hunter. She'd been home alone on the remote ranch when her nearest neighbour, Peter Mentone, paid an uninvited visit. Mentone had a history as a loner and a loser – he lived below the poverty line in a wooden shack with just a few cattle and his horse for company. He must have been seriously delusional if he expected the beautiful and respectable, married Marie to return the attention he was suddenly paying.

The journalist had done his research thoroughly. He recorded how Mentone had made his move, how Marie had fought back but couldn't stop the assault. She was left with bruises all over her body and a broken arm. So imagine the relief she felt when her husband, Robert Hunter, came home unexpectedly and caught Mentone in his kitchen raping his wife.

This is the graphic part. Court records told how Hunter broke the bolt on his own front door and crashed into the room. He saw Marie on the rug with Mentone still on top of her. He ran and grabbed the guy by the back of his jacket and swung him aside, not seeing the gun in Mentone's belt. I guess he was blind with rage as he sent him sprawling across the room. He stooped over his wife to help her up, then he turned to deal with her attacker.

Mentone had had time to get to his feet and draw the gun. He pointed it at Hunter and shot him in the head at point-blank range.

It was an open-and-shut case. Mentone had killed his victim and fled the scene, but Marie soon identified him and the sheriff arrested him – he was hiding stupidly in his shack. He didn't try to run or resist in any way. They had the trial and they hung Mentone within two weeks of the crime.

No one felt sorry – Robert Hunter had been well liked and his wife had been brought up by a strict protestant family in the town. She'd taught school before she married and settled down.

There was another tragedy for Marie Hunter to bear, the journalist added. Nine months after the rape and the death of her husband, she gave birth to a child – a baby girl whom she named Hester after the girl in a classic novel by Nathaniel Hawthorne.

I was stunned by the report and sat for what seemed

like an age running through the details. I got through to the end of the account for a fourth time. Mentone had raped Marie and she had his baby! Plus, Hunter had a first name – Robert. He wasn't only Hunter the overlord with the fading angel-wing tattoo.

While I was staring out of the window working through my reaction, Brandon Rohr rode up on his Harley.

He came into the café, straight to my table. 'Coffee,' he called to the waitress.

'Hey, Brandon, is this a weird coincidence or what?' I set up the ironic defence before he could, overcoming the spooky feeling that he was stalking me. 'Sit down, why don't you?'

'Darina.' Unzipping his leather jacket, he didn't seem in the mood to take up the challenge. 'We don't see you this side of town. What happened?'

'I wanted a quiet morning to focus on a school project. It was working until you walked in through the door – thanks!'

'I'm out of here,' he offered. And he meant it. He picked up his keys and scraped back his chair.

'No, stay. Drink your coffee.' I looked more closely and dropped the stalker theory. Brandon seemed tired, minus the usual macho posturing. 'How are you doing?'

'Good,' he said, walking over to the counter to save the

waitress a trip. He stayed there to sip his coffee.

'What happened to you?' I asked. 'How come you're not pressing my buttons?'

'I'm not in the mood.'

'You were the last time we met, outside the Madisons' place.' This new subdued Brandon allowed me past the tough-guy image to view the Brandon that reminded me more of Phoenix – quiet and somehow vulnerable. 'Really – did something bad happen?'

He came back to the table, turned his chair around and sat astride. 'The cops brought Zak home,' he told me. 'Last night. They caught the kid setting fire to a janitor's store at his school.'

'That's bad. I'm sorry.'

'Mom went crazy. After she yelled at Zak she turned on me and said it was all down to me. Zak needed someone he could look up to and now Phoenix is gone, I'm the lousy role model he has to follow.'

'She said that? So when did you last set fire to a janitor's store?' I asked. Phoenix had told me about Brandon's past and it didn't include arson. True, there was a jail sentence for fighting over a girl and beating the other guy to a pulp, and other angry adolescent stuff before that. But nothing since, as far as I knew.

'You know what Mom means,' he muttered. 'I need to

set Zak an example the way Phoenix did.'

'So the pressure's on. What exactly does she want you to do?'

'Rewind ten years, wipe the exam failures, the gangs, the fights, the conviction for assault, you name it.' The bitter tone told me he was way down in a deep hole, not even trying to climb out.

'Seriously – what can you do?'

'Ditch the Harley, get work, be home nights.' Drinking the dregs of his coffee, Brandon slammed the cup down. 'You know what she wants, Darina? She wants me to do what Phoenix did, she wants me to act like him, look like him – she wants me to *be* him!'

Sleep was a million miles away. I lay in my bed that night, my mind going a hundred miles per hour, flipping from one topic to another.

First, the copycat killing in Florida. I tried to stand back from my first thought of *Hey, it's the same guy!* Slow right down. Run that through again. I took a deep breath and told myself that Florida was half a continent away. Crazy gunmen usually stayed local. They had their killing spree then ran home and holed up, went back to living their lives with no one even suspecting the guy who lived above the convenience store or the loner who drove the animal-feed truck – until they went out and shot more innocent people.

But then I remembered the same quick getaway technique, the identical calculating mind behind the two crazy acts. Whoever shot Summer and the Venice victims must have planned the whole thing in advance. And the white baseball cap stuck in my mind, even amongst the whirl of warring ideas.

I turned and pulled the blankets over my head, trying to stop the muscles in my legs from twitching and to get some sleep.

And what about Hunter? How could I look at him in the same way now that I'd read exactly what happened to him and Marie? There was a rape and then there was a daughter. How had Marie handled the disgrace of that back then? Had she given Mentone's baby up for adoption? Had she lived the rest of her life hanging her head in shame?

And Hunter had a first name. He was an actual rancher with a Christian name, who died trying to save his wife from a rapist. Imagine the worst thing that could happen to a guy and it had happened to him out at Foxton more than a century ago.

I turned again, pummelled my pillow back into shape. Maybe I should turn on the light and read a magazine because I sure wasn't going to sleep. I reached out for the lamp switch.

It was right at that moment that Phoenix appeared. My hand was stretched out, my fingers were feeling for the switch. A wind blew in through the open window, the drapes billowed and he stood there in a halo of silver light.

Phoenix was with me the whole night. Hunter had sent him and said he should stay until morning.

It was like a gift, all my Christmases and birthdays rolled into one, to have my Beautiful Dead boyfriend lying by my side.

'This can't be happening,' I whispered. The fantastical silver light had faded – he was solid flesh, though hardly visible as we lay together. But I reached out to touch him and knew every contour of his face – smooth forehead, long lashes, full, soft lips.

'Don't talk,' he sighed. 'Hold me.'

'What happened? Are you OK?'

'Don't talk.' He kissed me and held me as if he thought someone would come, something bad would happen and I would be snatched away.

'It's OK,' I breathed, stroking his thick dark hair. 'I'm here.' And to convince him I kissed his lips, his closed eyelids, his cheeks. I held his hands and guided them across my own face, felt them tremble as he stroked my neck. Then I arched into him and sank in the moment, letting him know how much I loved him.

* * *

70

We tried everything we knew not to see the dawn sun in the sky.

'Close the curtains,' Phoenix murmured. 'Don't let the light in.'

The darkness had dissolved enough for me to see his face beside me. He was lying on his stomach, head turned towards me. Folding back the blanket, I ran my hand down the smooth skin of his back and rested it over his angel-wing tattoo. 'I love to look at you,' I whispered back.

After a while, Phoenix raised himself and leaned on one elbow, gazing down at me. 'You want to know why Hunter let me be here?'

I shook my head. 'I don't want to talk about him.'

'To warn you again not to come out to Foxton until you get more information.'

'He already told me that!' I pretended to push Phoenix off balance and smiled when he collapsed on to me.

'Yeah. But he has spies everywhere. He has Donna and Iceman over here in Ellerton.'

'Watching me?' I knew the Beautiful Dead could be present but invisible, keeping silent watch. 'They might at least have let me know.'

Phoenix smiled back. 'Donna said you researched some information about a killing in Florida. She reported back to Hunter. He said the link wasn't strong enough, then sent me here.'

'To tell me I'd failed,' I sighed. 'But I'm not complaining. I'll take you as his messenger any day!'

Phoenix cut short my kiss by sliding his fingers between our lips. 'He didn't do it out of the goodness of his heart,' he reminded me.

'Because he doesn't have one,' I agreed. 'I know. So why did he let you come? Did you ask him?'

'Would it make any difference if I had?'

'Not to Hunter. But it would to me.' I broke free of him and lay on my back, staring at the ceiling. 'Did you beg him to let you see me? Did you tell him you couldn't keep away a single minute longer? Tell me you did!'

'Seriously? No – what I said was, I was worried about you.'

'Don't be.' I leaned over again and tried to smooth away the frown lines on Phoenix's forehead. 'I've done this before, remember – for Jonas and Arizona.'

The frown stayed where it was. 'This time it's different. The guy who shot Summer didn't aim before he fired. It was totally random. We're not looking for a sane explanation here.'

'So you stress about what I'm getting myself into? Me too, if I'm honest. But I'll take good care, believe me.'

'And if it gets too scary, you'll tell me?'

Looking up into his blue-grey eyes, which stared so intensely and read every beat of my heart, I murmured that I would call for help whenever I needed it.

'It won't always be me,' he warned. 'But this time Hunter agreed for me to come because I explained that I also wanted to talk to you about Zak.'

I nodded slowly. 'You heard about him starting the fire?' I felt a small stab of disappointment that it wasn't just for my sake that Phoenix was here in my bed.

'Dean told me. He listened in to your conversation with Brandon.'

'Jeez, Phoenix!' Was there nothing that the Beautiful Dead didn't know? 'So what else did Dean tell you?'

'Don't be mad, Darina.' He got up from the bed and went to close the curtains, throwing the room back into shadow. 'Dean discovered there were two other kids with Zak – they were a couple of years older. It's not an excuse for my brother, but it seems they dragged him along.'

'Will the cops understand that?'

He shrugged. 'Maybe. If he has someone to speak up for him. Brandon can't do it.'

'Brandon's in a bad place right now – but, yeah, you already know that. So your mom will look after Zak, won't she?'

'She'll try. All I'm saying is, now that I'm not around, Zak needs all the help he can get.' Phoenix sat on the bed, his back towards me, waiting for my reaction.

'I hear you,' I murmured. I was mesmerized by the death mark beneath his shoulder blade, the cruel reminder that we were always and for ever running out of time. I slid down from the bed and knelt beside him, resting my head in his lap. 'When do you have to leave?'

He stroked my cheek. 'Now,' he said, his voice faded to almost nothing. 'I love you, Darina. Always, even after I'm gone – always remember that.'

I planned to make it into school that day for a Summer concert rehearsal, so after Phoenix dematerialized I showered, dressed and went downstairs.

Laura and Jim were in the kitchen, getting ready to start their own working days. They both looked up, but, unlike my mom, Jim didn't have it in him to hide his surprise. 'What happened, Darina? How come you're out of bed before midday?'

'Ha-ha.' I took my jacket off the hook by the door, making sure my keys were in the pocket.

'You're going to school?' Laura checked.

'It's Monday, so yeah.' They should be pleased – most Mondays lately I'd asked Laura to call in to say I was sick.

But today Logan had texted me to say that Miss Jones had called a major run-through. I went into the TV room to collect my guitar, then headed out.

'So you decided to play in the concert?' Laura called after me. Again, she shouldn't have stated the obvious and she should have sounded more pleased.

'Catch you later,' I called as I got into my *zoom-zoom* Brandon-mobile.

At school it was easier than I'd expected to mingle and keep a low profile. Nobody stared at me with their jaws open, saying, 'Hey, Darina, what are you doing here?' They just acted like I hadn't taken any time off – even the teachers.

Logan greeted me at the main door and walked into the building with me. 'Rehearsal is at twelve-thirty,' he reminded me. 'See you there.'

Hannah was in the classroom with Christian, Lucas and the techies, Parker and Ezra. She saw my guitar case and came across to talk about the 'Red Sky' duet we had planned.

By the start of the first class I felt as if I'd never been away.

'Hey, Darina – good job,' Ellerton High's music teacher, Katie Jones, said when we got to lunchtime and I walked into rehearsal. 'Just so you know – I put you and Hannah in as item number four on the programme, right after Logan's guitar solo. Also, I'd like you to be a backing singer on the song after the interval. Christian's going to sing the "Invisible" number. How do you feel about that?'

'Cool,' I told her. It felt good to sit and tune my guitar in the big, high-tech theatre that the school had built from its generous performing arts budget. Good too to be part of the crowd all getting together to celebrate Summer's music.

We started the rehearsal with Logan's solo. I liked to watch him sitting with his acoustic guitar, his whole focus on the instrument. He played well, not brilliantly, as Arizona's dad had once pointed out to me. Logan's technique was like the rest of him – solid and without too much flair, Frank Taylor had said. The guy was an expert musician so he should know. Anyway, I thought Logan did great and I clapped along with everyone else.

At the end of his piece Miss Jones moved in with her comments and Christian handed me the music for the backing vocals on 'Invisible'. 'Summer probably played you this track a thousand times,' he reminded me. 'You'll be singing with Jordan. Are you cool with that?'

'Totally.' The faint flavour of sympathy in Christian's voice made me move away, almost bumping right into

Parker Simons, who was carrying a heavy spotlight stand and a coil of thick cable. 'Why shouldn't I be?' I asked Christian over my shoulder.

Parker got out of my way and I went to join Hannah, who was sitting halfway up the tiered auditorium with her laptop. 'Let's find a corner to rehearse,' I suggested.

'Sit down. Let me finish here.'

Glancing across, I saw that she was working on improving an ad for the concert to put on the angelvoice website. Now that I thought about it, I recalled that Hannah had put herself in charge of the pre-concert marketing

'How many tickets have we sold?' I asked.

'Hundreds already. I was talking to Miss Jones about extending the gig from the one we've planned for the Saturday morning to a second one in the afternoon.'

'Cool.' I sat with my feet up on the seat in front, taking in the buzz of the theatre. 'Summer would love this,' I murmured. The musicians, the techie guys like Parker and Ezra, the gathering together of all this talent.

'Take a look at this.' Hannah tilted her screen towards me and let me read some recent comments on Summer's website.

Just bought my Summer tribute ticket – can't wait!

Listening to Summer's 'Red Sky' track – so-o-o sad!

I downloaded 'Invisible' and listened to it all nite long. Summer Madison rocks!

Mostly they were comments from girl fans, but I noticed one from a guy called JakB. *Summer lives on!* it said. *Her music is bigger than Death!* Instead of entering his own picture alongside his name, he'd used an icon of a fluorescent-green death's head. I pursed my lips and pointed it out to Hannah.

'Yeah, that's a little weird,' she agreed.

I scrolled down and found another JakB entry. *I know what it's like to be invisible,* he said. *Like the words of Summer's song – you're into a girl but she doesn't notice you. It sucks.* Then he typed out the chorus: 'Every day / You look my way / But I'm not there / I'm invisible . . .'

As it happened, this linked in with Christian standing onstage rehearsing the same section of the song. Hannah grabbed back her laptop and Jordan came looking for me. 'Darina, we're on!' she said, pulling me down the steps on to the stage.

I stayed in school for three whole days, mainly for the concert rehearsals but also to balance the secret work I was doing for the Beautiful Dead.

Darina, you're fixated, I told myself after a three-hour session early Wednesday evening in which I updated my reading of Summer's website reviews – more, much more from JakB, I noticed – and then searched the net for more Columbine-style killings that fitted the Ellerton and Venice, Florida models.

I found a depressing number of young guys with unhealthy loner habits and an even weirder interest in firearms – random shootings in malls, schools and colleges were nationwide and all too frequent. Usually though, the gunman martyred himself in the crossfire from a hail of bullets, which cut back big time on possible live suspects for the Summer homicide. I found only one other in the past two years where enough elements were similar – a shooting at yet another mall in New Jersey, where again the killer drove clean away.

It was something, but I knew Hunter would still want more, so I was glad of the interruption when Logan knocked on my front door and I went to let him in.

'Hey,' he said, making himself cosy at my kitchen table, just like the old days.

'Hey.' I got him a Coke from the fridge and sat down opposite. We dived straight into discussing details of the concert, then pretty soon strayed into less safe territory.

'Summer should be here,' I sighed, after Logan told me he was now note perfect on his solo. 'We're celebrating her music, her words – all we need is for her to be still with us.'

Logan took my hand across the table and I let him. He didn't say anything. His hand felt broad and warm and comforting.

'Did you know Laura sent me to see a therapist,' I told him suddenly.

Logan shook his head. 'How is it?' he asked.

'Cool. Her name is Kim Reiss. I like her. I shouldn't be telling you this.'

'Why? Haven't we known each other for ever?'

I nodded. 'You'll think I'm crazy.'

'So what's new?'

'Thanks, Logan! I sit in my therapist's yellow room on her leather couch and stuff comes pouring out – how I feel my life's spinning out of control, how I'll never reach where I want to be, somewhere safe with people I love.'

'That's not crazy. We all want that,' he said quietly, still holding my hand across the table.

I *had* known him for ever, which is why I went too far along this route. 'It started when my dad left home. I don't understand – how could anyone do that, break up a family that way?'

'I hear you. You were twelve years old.'

'So how come I couldn't stop him? Didn't he love me? Well, I guess not, or he'd stay in touch. I don't hear from him, did you know?'

'Maybe it's too hard for him.'

'Too hard?' Disbelief didn't cover my reaction. I stared at Logan as if he was the one who'd done the deserting.

'Some guys can't do it – the visiting, the saying goodbye each time.'

I took a deep breath. 'So again – why did he leave in the first place? I was twelve, for chrissake. And now Phoenix – gone!' I made a sudden swerve into the red danger lane.

'Don't cry.' Logan stayed where he was, except he put his other hand over mine. 'Darina, don't.'

'You know the problem? I'm left wanting what I know I can't have. That's what hurts. Happy families, Darina? No chance. Staying with the guy you love? Sorry, not in your script. Tell me, Logan – what happened to the future Phoenix and I had together?'

'All your dreams got shattered,' Logan whispered. 'One minute he was there, the next he was gone.'

I was sobbing now. *'It's not that simple,'* I wanted to tell him. *'I have to tell you – Phoenix came back from beyond the grave. He's out at Foxton with Summer right now right this second. They're the Beautiful Dead!'*

But Hunter sent in the storm troopers. The kitchen door blew open and slammed against the wall. I was blasted by an army of beating wings, which Logan couldn't hear, and by a bank of death heads building up in the room, black eye sockets gaping, teeth grinning, sweeping down on me until I almost suffocated.

Logan got up quickly to shut the door.

'No, no!' I pleaded, getting to my feet and stumbling out on to the porch. The skulls were smothering me. I was hyperventilating, putting my arms over my head to protect myself.

Logan came after me and grabbed hold of me. He held me tight until the panic was over. 'I'm here for you,' he promised. 'I won't ever let you down.'

That Friday I talked to Kim about my father. 'He left us for a woman named Karli Hamilton. Laura says she was the Barbie type. How shallow is that?'

'It's all about loss,' Kim told me. 'What you're going through right now with Phoenix and Summer, what happened with your father – the emotion you're dealing with on all these occasions is grief.'

Phoenix! After the death-head warning of Wednesday, alarm bells rang and I stayed well away from that topic.

Instead Kim and I talked through my early, pre-teenaged trauma and I came out believing maybe I wasn't responsible for my dad dumping me and Laura, which in some weird way had gotten etched into my brain right from the start. 'You didn't do anything wrong,' Kim told me clearly. And with that weight off my shoulders I left her office feeling lighter, a little easier in my mind.

After the session I was heading straight into school for an afternoon rehearsal but I got diverted because while I was driving through town I saw Zak Rohr hanging out with a couple of older kids outside the gas station where Phoenix had died. I pulled right over and leaned out.

'Why aren't you in school?' I asked him, sounding like Jim'n'Laura and with Phoenix's words ringing in my ears – 'Zak needs all the help he can get.'

Zak shot me a look of contempt. His buddies made nasty signals in my direction.

'Get in the car,' I told him. 'We need to talk.'

I guess Zak was partly swayed by the temptation of a ride in my shiny red car. He hesitated and tried not to lose face, but a couple of seconds later he was opening the passenger door and sliding on to the cream leather seat. 'Cradle snatcher!' his buddies jeered at me as I drove off. Einsteins they were not.

'So, did you start any more fires lately?' My idea as I

drove Zak out of town was to get down to basics.

He turned down the corners of his mouth then slouched further down into the deep seat. 'Why did Brandon give you this car?' he wanted to know.

'Because my old one broke.'

'So?'

'So he looks after me, I guess.'

'How come?'

'Because of Phoenix.'

'Crap,' Zak grunted. 'Mom's car broke. Brandon didn't buy her a new convertible.'

'He got this car from a guy he knows. I don't know if money was involved – maybe the guy owed your brother a favour.' We left the urban road and headed out to Hartmann Overlook where I knew we could park and continue our talk. It was good to leave the houses behind and feel the wind in our hair.

'Listen, Zak, I want to help you.'

'Can you get the cops off my back?' he demanded, assuming the familiar Rohr position of leaning back in the seat and resting his feet up on the dashboard. In fact though, when I looked closely he was no junior version of Phoenix. He had lighter hair and brown eyes and, at thirteen, he was still scrawny, with that awkward thin-wrists-big-hands adolescent thing going on.

'I can try,' I told him. 'Give me a name.'

'Jardine. He's deputy sheriff.'

I made a mental note and carried on. 'Is he planning to charge you?'

'Maybe. Jacob says they don't have the evidence.'

'Jacob is one of those guys back at the gas station?'

Drawing his sunglasses out of his jacket pocket, Zak put them on to improve the match with Phoenix. It struck me that he was doing this on purpose – deliberately identifying with his dead big brother. I even had a suspicion that these were Phoenix's own glasses. 'Jacob set the fire. I stood by with Taylor and watched.'

'Did you try to stop him?'

Zak shrugged and waited for me to turn off the road at the overlook. Behind his shades and with his feet still up, he succeeded in looking downright unimpressed with the panoramic view of mountains and lake. He changed the subject, back to what interested him. 'So Phoenix told Brandon to take care of you,' he guessed.

My heart missed a beat and I gripped the steering wheel. 'Yeah,' I admitted. 'That's pretty much the way it was.'

'When he lay dying?'

I winced, then nodded.

'So Brandon doesn't want you to be his girl?'

I couldn't help letting out a sudden yelp of laughter at Zak's naivety. 'Do I look like Brandon's type?' Brandon Rohr rode a Harley and wore fringed leathers. He never smiled or used words with more than two syllables.

'Mom says yes. She figures Brandon wants to step into Phoenix's shoes.'

It was time for a deep breath. 'Tell her no way. Brandon is so last century.' I watched Zak's lips curl upwards and a slow smile formed. 'Wait until he hears what you just said!'

'Yeah, tell him from me, just in case your mom's theory is correct.' That should kill any ideas Brandon might have. Again I switched topics. 'So you miss Phoenix as much as I do, right?'

'Every minute,' he admitted, suddenly going young and vulnerable on me. 'Without him around, my family is falling apart.'

'So come and find me when you need to talk,' I said at last. It was time to turn on the engine and get back on the road. 'School's over for the week. I'll drive you home.'

I made the rehearsal thirty minutes late, in time to sing my 'Red Sky' number with Hannah. Miss Jones reminded us all that we were only two weeks away from performing the concert on the anniversary of Summer's death. Two weeks also for me to solve the murder.

'Where were you?' Jordan asked me as we sat watching the lighting guys work out cues for the big finale number. She told me I'd already missed the run-through of our 'Invisible' routine with Christian.

'I was child-minding Zak Rohr. He cut school so I drove him home.'

Jordan's eyebrows shot up. 'Didn't you tell me that his mom zaps you with hate rays every time you go near?'

'Yeah. But I feel responsible for Zak, don't ask me why. Anyhow, I dropped him at the door and drove away before she had time to come out of the house. Did we persuade Miss Jones to add an extra performance?' I was getting good at this sudden switch of focus, away from stuff I didn't want to discuss.

'She said no, it's not appropriate because the afternoon is when Summer actually died,' Jordan answered. 'The same with the evening – people will want to mourn in private. We do one morning concert, period. The tickets are already sold out.'

All tickets sold! Early on Saturday morning I clicked on to the angelvoice website and found that Jordan was right. Clicking again on the Comments and Reviews icon, I read that many of Summer's fans were truly disappointed, including the fixated JakB guy who kept on popping up with his green skull icon.

This sucks, he complained. *I came online to buy my ticket as soon as I could raise the dough. But too late already. Is this what you do to a genuine fan? I love Summer Madison more than the whole world!!!*

Get a life! I thought, moving quickly on. A whole weekend opened up in front of me and I badly wanted to find something that would allow me out to Foxton again. I went back on to the Ellerton History of Violence site then followed it through to the Summer Madison shooting and made the link to the copycat situation in Florida, where I found some new information that surprised me. *Venice Killings linked to Pennington tragedy,* I read in an article from a New Jersey paper dated thirteenth April. *Police investigators have compared the Florida shooting in June last year with an incident here in New Jersey on September fifteenth. The Pennington victim was also shot at close range in an apparently random attack. A police source confirms that other similar killings across America are now under close scrutiny.*

I scrolled back and made myself re-read every word. Was it enough? Could I drive out to the ridge and show Hunter the development? Wait – there was more. I clicked on to a follow-up article dated next day, April fourteenth.

Venice Suspect Identified. The headline jumped off the screen at me. There was a name – Scott Fichtner – and a head-and-shoulders mugshot of a thin-faced, fair haired guy staring straight at camera.

I looked closely. Could it be the guy I'd seen at the mall, behind the aviator shades, beneath the baseball cap? He had the same thin face and long jaw, and he was the right kind of age.

The newspaper told me that Scott Fichtner was a twenty-year-old college dropout born in Brooklyn who left home aged eighteen and went to study music at Miami State. He stayed until halfway through his first semester then disappeared from view. There was one conviction for underage drinking, another for a small-time drugs offence. Now, it seemed, the cops had enough evidence to link him with at least two homicides – Venice and Pennington – and to blast his photograph across the news media.

OK, that was all I needed to know. I printed off the details plus the photograph and stuffed them in my pocket. I didn't tell Jim where I was going – why break an ingrained habit? I was out of the house and in my car. It was ten in the morning and I was driving out to Foxton, determined this time to show Summer the picture and convince Hunter that Scott Fichtner was well and truly in the frame.

I did all the right things. I kept to the speed limit through Centennial, I checked my mirror to make sure no one was following me. When I parked my car under the aspens on Foxton Ridge, I put it out of sight behind a rock. So I expected the last part of my journey to go smoothly. I would walk along the ridge until I reached the water tower, by which time the Beautiful Dead would have used their super-sensitive hearing to pick up my presence. Hunter would send someone up to meet me.

Make it Phoenix! I said to myself, picturing another happy reunion under the midday sun.

In spite of what had occurred last time, I wasn't ready for what actually happened.

First I heard the rustle of wind through the new leaves and felt it blow against my light shirt and through my hair. Like a fool I welcomed it and walked another ten paces. The wind picked up. It flattened the grass on the hillside leading down to the barn, making waves of movement that built up until it reached me and almost knocked me off my feet.

'Hey!' I cried. I raised my arms and yelled like a crazy girl down into the valley. 'It's me, Darina!'

I guess the wind drowned me out. It grew stronger and turned again into my worst nightmare – the sound of wings battering my eardrums, rising to a monstrous roar even though I put my hands over my ears and begged for it to stop. Then the wings grew so loud they were inside my head, and the sky darkened and the death-head apparitions blocked out the sun.

'It's me!' I yelled. 'I'm alone. I have something to show you!'

But it kept on coming, this heavy barrier beating me back, making me bend almost double as I tried to resist.

Any stranger, any far-siders experiencing this for the first time would have caved in. The skull vision would have got inside their heads along with the beating wings. Reality would have dissolved, the dizzying nightmare would have taken over. This was how the Beautiful Dead preserved their secret life on Foxton Ridge.

But I alone knew they were there and I refused to give in. At the risk of Hunter blasting my memory a second time, I would go on my hands and knees, I would crawl forward inch by inch all the way down that hill until I reached the house and the barn.

The wings beat on and the skulls whirled. I tore my shirt on a thorn bush. When I reached the razor-wire fence, a gust of wind tore into me, throwing me sideways and over a ledge into a dry gulley.

I landed hard on my back, staring up at a figure I didn't recognize at first.

'Hunter told you not to come back,' a guy's voice said, cold as ice.

The legs straddled the gulley and the face was in shadow, but I knew it wasn't Iceman, and it definitely wasn't Phoenix. 'Who is that? Is it you, Dean?' I asked, trying to raise myself on one elbow.

The new member of the Beautiful Dead reached forward and thrust me back down like I was vermin. He kept me pinned on my back by the force of his gaze alone. 'It's my job to keep far-siders out,' he muttered.

'Not me!' I groaned, lying in the dirt. I knew it wasn't worth trying to get up again until Dean decided to let me. 'I'm on your side.'

'I know that. But the order was to keep everyone out, you included.'

'I don't have time for this.' I tried to push against

Dean's invisible hold, but again I fell back helpless. 'Did Hunter mean me? Did he actually mention my name?'

'You got it.' The voice was flat and world weary, the shadowy face unreadable.

'OK, so you did a good job, now let me get up.' This was crazy; I was seriously angry. 'I said, let me get up!'

'The order was to keep everyone out,' Dean repeated. 'And if anyone tried to break through the barrier, my order was to send that person right back where they came from.'

'No, wait!' Desperately I tried to raise my hand to shield my head, as if by doing that I could stop him wiping my memory clean. I knew all too well that this was a second offence and that this time I would stay wiped. 'Don't do it. Summer is short of time, her twelve months is almost up. She needs me – don't zap me, please!'

Dean leaned forward again, this time to seize me by the wrist and drag me upright into the whirl of beating wings. 'I can get right inside your head,' he reminded me, drawing me to within centimetres of his face. 'I can see every thought in there.'

'Then you know I won't do anything to harm the Beautiful Dead,' I cried. 'You can see I love Phoenix more than the world!'

Dean's gaze burned into me, he held me helpless and

squirming, deciding whether or not to rob me of the memories I clung to and toss me back into the world like a piece of flotsam from a wrecked ship.

Another voice broke the terror of that moment. 'Let her go,' Donna told him. 'Hunter says to bring her down to the barn.'

I'd asked Donna for an explanation and got no answers. All she did was to clutch the collar of her long woollen coat tight around her throat as she led me and Dean down the hill and across the yard, leaving us at the open barn door.

'This isn't about me,' I tried to tell him. 'I came to help Summer.'

Dean stared blankly back at me, a typical ex-cop – square-shouldered, square-jawed, bone-headed, silent.

'Don't you know how little time she has left? Two weeks! The clock is ticking here!'

Still he gave me nothing back.

'So what do we do now?' I demanded. I stood in the glaring sun, looking round and hoping to see Phoenix stride out of the house or across the meadow.

Instead, it was Hunter, stooping as he came out through the front door then standing legs apart on the porch, fingers hooked into his jeans pockets, staring coldly at me. 'I hope this isn't a social visit,' he said.

I wanted to yell at him: 'Look at my shirt, look what this goon did to me!' But you didn't yell at Hunter, you waited for his next move.

'Good job, Dean,' he said as he stepped down from the porch. 'You see how it works?'

Dean nodded. 'It's neat. No sane person can stand up to that kind of treatment.'

'No, they always turn and run,' Hunter agreed. 'They get home with a sore head and no clue as to what happened out here.'

'Hold it!' I couldn't help it, I had to speak out. 'What am I, some kind of experiment that Dean gets to test out his supernatural powers on?'

Hunter had joined us by the barn door. He narrowed his eyes and did his telepathy thing on me, making me step back and look down at the ground. 'Yeah, Darina, you're an experiment, a work in progress.'

'And what about Dean? Where exactly does he fit in?' Dean wasn't like the other Beautiful Dead – he was way older for a start.

Hunter considered his answer carefully. 'Firstly, Dean holds information specific to Summer's case, and that could be useful to us,' he explained. 'Second, he steps into my shoes when I'm done here. Meanwhile, there's a whole lot for him to learn.'

'When you're done . . . ?' I faltered, my gaze flicking from one man to the other. 'That makes Dean an overlord, like you?'

'An overlord like me.' Hunter smiled at my confusion. 'You thought I was the only one and that I was around for ever?'

'For as long as Phoenix and the others needed to come back to the far side,' I admitted. What I was feeling was a strange sort of panic. True, Hunter scared the hell out of me and angered me and always stood in the way between me and Phoenix, but I also felt a bond with him that I didn't want to loosen.

'Not true,' he said. 'I take orders too.'

Who from? Who told Hunter when his job was done? What happened then? Was he trapped in limbo without ever knowing exactly what had taken place between his wife and Peter Mentone?

'You brought something to show me?' he asked, following my thoughts and swiftly forcing things onwards.

I didn't bring out the picture of Fichtner right away, I was still too mad about my hostile reception. So I dug in my heels and stayed with the discovery I'd made about Mentone, plus the stuff about Marie's baby girl, Hester.

'I've been doing some work,' I muttered. 'It's crazy what you can find on the net.'

Hunter read my thoughts again and his eyelids flickered shut. Dean glanced at him with a worried frown.

'Stuff from way back,' I taunted. I admit I was enjoying seeing Hunter knocked off balance for once. 'Records from old murder cases, newspaper reports, you name it.'

Hunter looked up with a flash of anger in his steel-grey eyes. 'Darina, that's enough! Give me the picture.'

That flash had hit me like an electric shock and made me tremble as, helplessly, I pulled the photograph out of my pocket and handed it to Hunter. 'Scott Fichtner. He's linked to two shootings,' I muttered. 'The pattern of events is the same as what happened to Summer in Ellerton.'

As I spoke her name, she emerged from the shadows of the barn into the light. The sun caught her hair, shining gold against the palest, unblemished skin of her face and neck. Now that the weather had turned warmer, she was wearing a low-cut, sleeveless white shirt with sprigs of blue flowers, with a flowing dark-blue skirt that showed only her ankles and the silver strappy sandals on her feet. She looked so young as she walked towards me with an uncertain smile.

Hunter briefly studied the Fichtner picture then showed it to Dean. He gestured for Summer to join us.

'Share your new theory with Summer,' he instructed me.

Still trembling, I took a deep breath. 'There's a guy going around the country shooting people in shopping malls – one in Florida, one in New Jersey. Maybe he's our man, so I brought his photograph.'

Summer's eyes widened in her delicate face and she put up her hand to cover the dark angel-wing tattoo placed high above her heart on her death-white flesh. It was the first time I'd seen the death mark and it made me gasp.

'Take a look,' Hunter invited her. 'Do you recognize him?'

For Summer I could tell it was like stepping up to the executioner's block – to look at that picture, possibly to come face to face with her killer. All of a sudden I wanted to snatch the photo back and spare her the trauma. I took a quick step forward.

Dean stopped me with one of his clumsy, over-the-top zombie zaps. *Ouch!*

Hunter handed Summer the print of Scott Fichtner's photograph.

She never was able to conceal her feelings – her features were too fine and open, her responses too immediate. So I saw her eyelids flutter and her bottom lip quiver, I saw the look of pain in her violet eyes.

'Is it him?' Hunter asked.

She gasped again as if she was struggling for breath. Loosening her grip, she let the picture flutter to the ground and rest between her feet.

'Let me go to her!' I begged Dean, who kept me pinned to the spot.

Summer staggered sideways just as Phoenix came out of the barn. He caught her and swept her into his arms, carried her back into the barn while Hunter, Dean and I looked on.

Was I jealous? If I say that I was, does that make me a bad person?

I held the image of Phoenix gathering Summer up and it scrambled my brain. I was out of control, thinking a thousand unworthy thoughts.

I mean, Summer and Phoenix spent all their time together, they were both Beautiful Dead.

Hunter let me stew for a whole hour after Phoenix took Summer away. He put me on the porch with Dean then followed them into the barn, closing the door after him.

Dean sat with his feet up on the rail, his hands clasped across this stomach. I noticed his thick, hairy forearms, his blunt fingernails and glinting gold watchstrap. 'So Darina, you think you're on to something,' he said after

99

what seemed like a century of silence.

'I don't know. Maybe.'

'Scott Fichtner looks like our man, huh?'

'Maybe,' I said again.

'You reckon Summer recognized him and that's what made her drop to the ground?'

'He ticks the boxes,' I argued. I couldn't tear my thoughts away from Phoenix and Summer inside the barn. My gaze kept being drawn to the faded door with the moose head keeping glassy-eyed watch from above.

'You're talking serial killer,' Dean went on in an amused tone, like he'd seen a hundred homicides and I was the rookie cop. 'A kid obsessed with guns. He keeps a whole arsenal stashed in his grandparents' basement, he fantasizes about racking up a record number of victims before he finally turns the gun on himself and blows his own brains out.'

'That's sick, to joke about it like that,' I muttered. Truly, my stomach was turning.

'We're a sick society,' he reminded me. 'And I'm not exactly joking. But what if you're wrong, Darina?'

You don't know that I am,' I protested. 'You need to give Summer some time to study the picture and make up her mind.'

'You saw her killer, didn't you? Do *you* think Fichtner did it?'

'I only caught a glimpse – I can't be sure. But he shot Summer point blank, face to face – she would have got a better look.'

'That's supposing she can recall his face.' Dean spoke slow and flat, like he was discussing the contents of a grocery list. 'My guess is, she can't.'

'We don't *know* that!'

'Believe me – we do.' He let a long silence develop. 'So, suppose you're wrong and there's another possibility – maybe a local connection after all. And maybe not random.'

Up until this point I'd been leaning against the rail, but now I stood straight up, recalling Hunter's explanation that Dean had been brought in with information specific to Summer's case. 'How could it *not* be random? Summer had no enemies. No one in the world would want to harm her.'

'Take it easy,' Dean sighed. 'Think about it. For instance, think jealousy – you sure know all about that, Darina.'

'I'm not . . . you don't suppose . . . no way!' Glancing towards the barn, I spread my palms and spluttered a denial. 'You think I'm *jealous* of Summer!'

'Right now you're under the thumb of the green-eyed

monster. You're wondering what they're doing in there and how come Phoenix was right on the spot to save her.'

'Jeez!' I groaned, sitting on the chair next to him. 'I give up, Dean. I'm a heap of crap.'

For the first time a smile crept on to his face. 'You're a kid,' he said. 'You're allowed. So I'm about to give you a piece of advice. Not about Phoenix and Summer, and not about jealousy – I'm only a cop and that's not my territory. This is about Scott Fichtner.'

'And?' I prompted after another of Dean's heavy silences.

'I say it's a long shot. I reckon you should look closer to home. And I'm not saying Summer had enemies, though I do guess she had people who were jealous of her – the way she looks, the way she sings, the girl who had everything.'

'OK,' I said slowly.

'And a talented girl like her gets herself known. Fans download her music, they love her and want a piece of her, including all the crazies who creep out from under a stone.'

JakB! Summer's 'number one fan'. The idea hit me like a hammer blow to the head and I kicked myself for not thinking of this before.

'Am I right or am I wrong?' Dean asked, watching my face closely. 'And consider something else, a whole other theory. What if a gunman came into the mall with a specific other intention and Summer was just in the wrong place at the wrong time?'

'So we're back to the original random-shooting theory?' Ideas were crowding in now and I was already shelving my Fichtner suspicions for half a dozen new ones.

'It happens,' Dean insisted. Then he lowered his feet from the rail, stood up and walked slowly to the far end of the porch. 'You've been wondering exactly what I'm doing here, haven't you, Darina?'

'To shadow Hunter,' I said. 'To eventually step into his shoes.'

'But why now?'

'Because you were a cop,' I answered slowly.

He nodded. 'In Ellerton, at the time Summer was shot.'

'You worked on the case?' I came in fast this time, talking over him.

'No, I was on vacation. But I was back in the office a week later. I picked up a few pieces of information.'

'Something that would give us an actual lead?' All of a sudden I saw the whole picture, why Hunter had brought in Dean like he had.

'There were no clear trails,' he warned. 'But plenty of theories. Listen – I'm going to give you a name and I want you to talk to the guy, OK?'

'Tell me.'

'This is a uniformed officer who was on duty in the mall at the time of the shooting, and his name is Henry Jardine. You got that?'

'He's deputy sheriff,' I muttered. I recognized it straight away as the name Zak Rohr had dropped in – he was the cop who had handled the fire-setting incident.

'That's the guy. Look him up, Darina.'

I made a mental note – just in time, because I saw the barn door open and Phoenix walk out alone.

'Go,' Dean told me without looking round. He'd heard the creak of the door hinges. 'Go talk to your boyfriend, clear the air. But after that you go on home and you knock on Henry Jardine's door. And when you talk with him, you mention my name.'

'Walk with me,' Phoenix said.

He led the way down to the creek and we sat by the water, staring at the twisting eddies and sparkling reflections on the surface.

'I'm sorry,' I stammered. My self-worth had reached zero; I was wrecked by the effort not to give away

104

those bad, bad, jealous thoughts.

'What are you afraid of?' he asked, looking closely at me.

I was staring straight ahead at the cloud of white spring flowers just opened out amongst the sage bushes on the opposite bank, refusing to meet his eye.

'You already know,' I sighed.

'So tell me. Say it out loud.'

I looked at him at last and tears brimmed over. 'I'm scared, in spite of everything, you don't love me any more.'

'Because of what you saw back there by the barn? You think Summer and I . . . that there's some chemistry?'

I nodded and the tears trickled down my cheeks. 'I'm so sorry, Phoenix.'

Placing his fingers under my chin, he kept my face directed towards him.

'Summer and I have a heap of things in common,' he told me straight. 'I never really talked with her before, when we were both on the far side. There was no time to get to know her. But sure, we spend a lot of time together now.'

Oh God, my heart was sinking. I tried to steel myself for what was coming next.

'I'm totally in awe of her,' Phoenix said. 'How

105

can anyone not be?'

'She's amazing,' I whispered, trapped in the miserable, jolting certainty that Phoenix had fallen in love with Summer. 'Not just the obvious stuff, like her music and the way she looks, but I mean she's an amazing person.'

'Generous,' he agreed. 'And warm and funny – the total package.'

I shook my head and twisted away from him, waiting for the axe to fall. What would I do now? How could I go on?

'But,' Phoenix said, standing up then pulling me to my feet and keeping hold of both my hands. 'Baby, watch my lips – I do not love Summer Madison!'

Another shock wave went through my whole body.

'Darina, don't be scared,' he went on gently, his voice hardly audible. 'You know something? This is the first time I've wished you were one of us. You want to know why? Because if you were Beautiful Dead, right now you could read my mind.'

I closed my eyes for long, long seconds then took a deep breath and dared to look at him again. 'I wish the same thing. Often. In fact, every minute of every day I want to be with you, and for ever.'

He smiled sadly. 'That's how it is, if only you would believe me. Remember – I'll never let you go.'

I breathed in his words, absorbed them into my heart. 'I'm in school at a rehearsal and it looks like I'm into it, playing my part. But really my head is in a different space, out here at Foxton. I'm wondering where you are, what you're doing. I'm hoping you're not in danger.'

'Don't worry about me,' he murmured. He pulled me closer to him. 'I have supernatural powers, remember!'

'Yeah, *zap* – *kerpow!*' I tried to smile back but the tears kept on falling. 'I'm looking for you around every corner, waiting for you to materialize. I'm hating Hunter for not letting you.'

'And you're over this jealousy thing?' he checked. 'Or do you want to talk with Summer about it too?'

'No,' I said quickly. 'I'm over it!'

'So now it's my turn.' Phoenix ran his fingers through my hair, then took my hand to walk slowly upstream. Our feet brushed through the tender spring grass and small white and purple flowers. 'So I'm Superman but I have human weakness too.'

'Confession time!' I sighed. 'Go ahead, tell.'

'I think about you too – all the time. I'm wanting to know what you're doing, who you're with. Way out here in Foxton, sometimes there's no way I can know.'

'You have to wait until Hunter sends you?'

Phoenix nodded. 'He keeps me on a tight leash. There's

107

nothing I can do. Sometimes he sends Donna or Iceman – they report back that they've seen you at rehearsal for Summer's concert, or with Logan at your house.'

'Nothing happened!' I cried, much too fast. 'Logan held my hand and listened to stuff about my dad leaving home – that's it, end of story!'

'He held your hand?' This was news to Phoenix and he tried hard to swallow it. 'OK, good.'

'No, really. You were talking about the no-chemistry thing between you and Summer – that's the way I feel about Logan. I know he's a good guy and he'll always be there for me, and I'm grateful.'

'I hear you.' Phoenix tightened his hold on my hand and walked on.

'And you're cool with it?'

'I'm cool. Moving on – Iceman was there when Zak got in your car and you drove him home.'

'He's in trouble. I wanted to help.'

'Go to Brandon.' He paused and dug the toe of his boot into some loose pebbles, making them crunch and shift.

'Brandon has his own problems. He and your mom have been locking horns. But press Pause – go back to what you were saying about weaknesses.'

'It's crazy,' he sighed. 'I can look at you now and *see* you love me – it's in your eyes, your heart.'

'True,' I confirmed. It was my turn to take his hand and lead him forward.

'But I'm not really cool about Logan. When you're away from me, spending time with him, I get scared. And Christian and Lucas – there are a hundred guys out there waiting to hit on you.'

'Logan is my friend from way back – you know that. But zilch chemistry, like I said.'

'For you maybe,' Phoenix argued.

'And that's what counts.' I interrupted him because once and for all I wanted to settle this. 'You have to trust me and I have to trust you.'

We stood under an aspen tree, listening to the new leaves rustle overhead, enjoying the dappled light and shade.

'So we agree,' he murmured. 'No room for doubts?'

'Life's too short,' I whispered before I reached up and kissed him. 'Honestly – for us especially.'

I was on a permanent rollercoaster, up-down, up-down again with my emotions. Out at Foxton with Phoenix I was soaring over the heights, screaming with delight and hanging on for dear life. Back here in Ellerton, I was in the grey, murky depths.

'Your mom called your cell phone three times this morning,' Jim told me when he walked into the house with a stack of groceries. 'You never answered.'

'I guess I lost the signal,' I shrugged.

'So where were you?'

'What is this, are we living in a police state?'

'Laura worries about you. The least you can do is answer your phone.'

'I said I lost the signal.'

'She works too hard. The extra stress is bad for her.'

'Read my lips – I lost the signal!'

I guess I pushed him a centimetre too far. 'Darina, think about your mom for a change. Get past your own stuff and grow up!' Jim was red in the face, slamming packages onto shelves. It was the first time he'd yelled at me, ever, in five whole years.

'Believe me, that's what I was doing – ditching my problems, trying to help someone else.'

Jim shook his head.

'It's true. You want to know who? It's Zak Rohr, Phoenix's thirteen-year-old brother. The kid's in trouble with the cops.'

'I didn't know he had a kid brother.' My revelation made him take the volume down a little. 'Sure, I know about the older one, Brandon – he's bad news and that's one of the reasons why Laura stresses.'

'Because I see Brandon?'

'Yeah. Because he gave you the car. What's that about?'

I shrugged again. 'Why do I have to justify it? Brandon promised Phoenix he'd take care of me. What can I do?'

'Give the car back,' he suggested.

'And leave myself stranded? How do I get from A to B?'

'OK, so keep the car. But now you say the kid brother is following Brandon's bad example. What exactly did he do?'

'Nothing. He was there when a couple of older kids started a fire.'

'Jeez, Darina, that's perfect! Now the Rohrs are nurturing a crazy-boy arsonist.'

'Zak was in the wrong place at the wrong time. I spoke to him – he swears he didn't plan it or play any part.'

'And you believe him?'

'I do. I want to help him. Jim, you've driven a taxi, you hang out with a lot of the older guys in Ellerton. Do you know a cop called Henry Jardine?'

'Maybe. What does Jardine have to do with Zak Rohr?'

'He arrested the three kids outside the school janitor's office, where they set the fire.' Out of nowhere I was having a long conversation with my stepfather and it was going in the direction I wanted. If I played it carefully, I could pull off the difficult challenge of making direct contact with the cop Dean had told me about. 'What kind of a guy is he?'

'I hardly know him. I only met him through the fishing club we both go to.'

'A fly-fisher?' The sport was big around here, and I knew Jim spent his leisure time out at Hartmann Lake. 'He's cool then?'

'He's a regular guy and a big fisherman. Like I said, I

only see him at the lake. He's there most Sundays.'

This was good enough. 'Thanks, Jim,' I told him, heading upstairs to my room. 'And sorry about earlier. I'll call Mom right away.'

It's cool when I have a job to do, a new task to focus on, so I made a plan to drive out to Hartmann early next morning.

I mean, seriously early.

I was up with the dawn, creeping downstairs and out of the house before Laura and Jim were up, and I was dressed in cut-off denim shorts, Laura's two-sizes-too-big plaid shirt and her hiking boots, secretly borrowed from her closet. How cool did I look!

The thing was – I had to appear like a regular hiker who liked to catch the early bird. Could I do it? Maybe, if I smoothed down my hair and rolled up my sleeves. I refused to leave off the mascara though – I drew the line there. I drove out through Centennial, almost forgetting to take a right turn before I reached Turkey Shoot Ridge, so programmed was I into following the route to Foxton.

'Shoot!' I swung the wheel at the last moment, on to the dirt road leading to the lake. On the way I passed two Jeeps carrying groups of campers who were coming away from the National Forest camp ground. Neither gave way to my shiny red car and I ended up twice with two wheels in the ditch. On each occasion, my Summer Madison demo CD jumped out of its groove. I played it on a loop, making her the current soundtrack to my life.

'Red sky when you say goodbye/Red sky makes me cry/Forever.' I was singing out loud when I finally reached Hartmann, parked the car in the campsite car park alongside half a dozen SUVs and took a small shoulder pack from the trunk.

If I'm honest, this is the point where my detailed plan grew less detailed. I'd come looking for fishermen, and one in particular, so it made sense to make my way down to the lake shore where I saw figures dotted along the water's edge, each with a rod and a line. Of course, they were too far away to make out clearly, and in any case I didn't know what Henry Jardine looked like. So now which way did I go?

I was still hesitating when footsteps approached from behind.

'Darina?' It was Jon Madison speaking – he owned the footsteps and stopped in fake shock. 'My God, is it you or did my eyes just play tricks on me?'

'Funny, Mr Madison. Of course it's me.' I saw that he was carrying a big, old-time, non-digital camera, slung on a strap around his neck, and he was dressed in the same plaid shirt and hiking boots uniform as me.

'What are you doing out here?'

'Hiking,' I said with a frown. 'What does it look like?'

'Alone?' Still Summer's dad made like he couldn't believe what he saw. 'I didn't have you down as an outdoors kind of girl.'

I ignored him and stated the obvious. 'So you're taking photographs.'

'For Heather, actually. Hartmann is one of her favourite places.'

'She didn't come too?'

'No. Lately she's gone back to how she was after it first happened. We're coming up to the anniversary, so she's not strong enough to leave the house.'

'I'm sorry, Mr Madison.'

'Me too. Heather and Summer were the same – real sensitive, creative people. You just want to protect them from all the bad stuff in life. You know you can't, but it doesn't stop you trying.'

'I hear you.' I thought of Summer out at Foxton, the girl with the golden gifts. And of her mother, the faded, grief-stricken lady I'd seen at the party.

'Anyways, I had the idea that showing Heather pictures of the lake in the early spring will, you know,

115

revive her a little. She may even use the photographs to start painting from.'

'I hope you're right.'

'I have another thought.' He paused uncertainly. 'How would it be if you came to visit us again?'

'Would Heather be cool with that?' I asked, considering her response to seeing me in Summer's room during my birthday visit.

'I'm guessing yes. She talks about you, says it makes her feel closer to our daughter. So will you?'

I thought for a while, then nodded.

Jon Madison took a deep breath and forced a smile. 'Good. Call this evening then.'

'At six-thirty,' I promised.

'Don't let me hold up your hike, Darina. See you tonight.'

'Yeah, goodbye, Mr Madison.' I lurched off to my left, through bulrushes and reeds towards a willow thicket, not realizing that the soggy ground would suck me down.

'Watch out!' Summer's dad warned, too late.

Fifty metres further along the lake's edge, a fisherman flicked his line over his shoulder and then jerked it forwards, letting his reel unwind. I heard the whirring noise above the squelch and suck of my boots in the mud.

'Actually, I'm out here looking for someone!' I turned to confide in Jon Madison. 'Do you know Henry Jardine?' But this time it was me who was too late – Summer's dad had taken off in the opposite direction and didn't look round.

'You're looking for Henry?' The fisherman up ahead had overheard my question. 'You're out of luck. He's not here.'

Shoot again! I didn't have any backup to my crappy plan. 'Are you certain?' I checked with the old guy with the rod.

'Trust me,' he grunted. 'I see everyone arrive and leave. He's not here.'

So what could I do except turn around and squelch back towards the car park? My feet were already wet and the mud was oozing between my toes inside Laura's boots. When I reached dry land, I sat on a rock to unlace them, not even looking up at a newly arrived fisherman who passed close by. The boots and socks were laid out in a row to dry in the sun when I heard the old guy in the distance call out a greeting to the newcomer. 'Hey, Henry, did you talk with the girl?'

Now I looked up. I saw the back view of the new arrival – a middle-aged man in a grey T-shirt, wearing the long rubber waders that fishermen use, with a canvas pack slung from one shoulder and carrying a rod in his right hand. I sprang up from the rock and ran barefoot after him.

He turned towards me, obviously expecting trouble, concentrating his disapproval on my feet. Then, as I arrived, he looked me up and down. 'Do I know you?' he demanded.

'No. Yes! Well, not exactly. I was a witness at the Summer Madison shooting.'

'Honey, do you see me in uniform? Does it look like I'm on duty?' the deputy sheriff grunted, getting ready to walk right on.

I ran to block his path. 'You're Henry Jardine, right? You knew Dean, the cop who was killed in a road crash?'

This halted Henry in his tracks. He didn't let down this guard though – he kept his eyes narrowed. His drooping, dark, western-style moustache hid his mouth and stopped me reading his mood. 'What's Dean Dawson got to do with anything?' he asked.

'Nothing. He was a friend of yours?'

'So?'

'I . . . knew him. He shared a few theories with me about Summer's death. And no, before you ask, I don't have anything new to tell you about his crash.'

'And I'm still out of uniform,' Henry reminded me. But

he hung around long enough to show he was interested in what I was doing there.

'It's about Zak Rohr,' I told him.

Jardine swatted a fly that buzzed around his face. 'Zak who?'

'Rohr. You caught him setting a fire with two other kids, remember?'

'Oh, the Rohr family – they're a great addition to the Ellerton community.' He gave a hollow laugh and was about to walk on again. 'What happened to your shoes?' he asked as an afterthought.

'They're on the rock back there. Listen, I talked with Zak. He had nothing to do with the fire.'

'You're the girlfriend,' Jardine recalled all of a sudden. 'Phoenix Rohr had a girlfriend. He was planning on meeting you the night he got stabbed. Wait, I got the name on the tip of my tongue . . . Davina . . . Darina. Yeah, Darina!'

I could have praised Jardine's powers of recall, but decided against it. Instead, I let my shoulders sag at the mention of Phoenix's name.

'So now you're trying to help out the kid brother,' Jardine went on more kindly than I'd expected. 'But go figure – maybe he doesn't deserve your help.'

'I talked it through with him – the older kids—'

'Jacob Miller and Taylor Stafford,' Jardine interrupted.

'It was down to them. Zak was a pure spectator.'

'But he didn't try to stop them.'

'It was two bigger guys against one young kid – how could he?'

'I hear you,' Jardine said, turning me around and walking me back towards my footwear. 'I already got the number of Miller and Stafford, believe me.'

'So Zak is off your radar?' I felt hopeful enough to press for a straight answer.

'I'm writing a report,' was all Henry would say.

'Including the fact that Zak wasn't directly involved?'

'Let's say I didn't see him with the empty gas can or the lighter in his hand, and leave it at that. OK?' We stopped by the rock with my boots and socks steaming in the sun. 'I'm not handing out any promises,' Jardine added.

'Thanks,' I said anyway and let out a relieved sigh, sitting down to pull on my soggy socks.

He kept a watchful eye on me and ran a hand over his moustache. 'You pop right up in the centre of events, don't you, Darina? I'm not only talking about Zak Rohr – I mean, you've had some serious bad luck over the past twelve months. Witness to a shooting. Bereaved girlfriend. Anything else?'

'It's plenty,' I said quickly. 'On the Summer shooting – I

was actually wondering if there are any moves to follow up the arrest of Scott Fichtner?'

'Whoa!' Jardine put out his hands in protest then waved his arms as if he was stopping a runaway horse.

'Sorry,' I mumbled. 'I just read about it online.'

'And you jumped to a conclusion, huh?'

'I need to know what happened to Summer!' Suddenly I let it all hang out – my feeling of horror at what I'd witnessed, my sense of loss.

Jardine heard it in my voice and read it in my eyes. 'Come see me in my office,' he told me quietly. 'Tomorrow morning, early.'

'It's taking me a while, but I'm getting there,' I told Summer as I drove out to her parents' house in Westra.

She wasn't with me in the car, but I guessed the Beautiful Dead had set a spy on me, so I went ahead and talked. Somehow the message would get through.

'I'm following up the Fichtner connection,' I explained. 'Dean told me straight that you can't remember the face of the guy who shot you and I hear what he's saying. The others couldn't remember the details either – I mean, Jonas and Arizona. I understand about you blocking out the actual event – the trauma and everything. So the photograph of Fichtner didn't help – I get that.'

I stopped at a red light, glanced left, then when I looked right again, Phoenix was sitting beside me in his halo of silver light.

He looked straight at me, giving me his lopsided smile, saying nothing. God, he was beautiful!

The light turned green but I was too busy gazing at Phoenix to move forward. 'So cool!' I breathed.

He grinned at me. 'Flying visit.'

'Ha!' The driver behind me blasted his horn. 'Wait,' I told Phoenix as I eased through the lights, then off the road. 'If they don't let you use your cell phone while driving, they sure don't let you talk to the undead!'

'Do they allow talking to yourself or do they pull you over for being a crazy person?' He waited until I was safely parked, then drew me over. 'I've been watching you since you left home,' he explained between kisses.

'How long can you stay?' There were more kisses, before, during and after my question.

'Really, this is a flying visit. Hunter wants an update.'

'Tell him I spoke to Henry Jardine. I have an official meeting with him tomorrow at his office. I'm guessing he'll put Scott Fichtner into the frame for us.'

'So we really are getting close to an answer.' Phoenix pulled away from me so that he could see me more clearly. 'Summer needs good news. She's having a hard time right now.'

'So is her mom. It's the anniversary coming up – Jon Madison says she can't handle it.'

'Summer is so fragile. She's scared there'll be more violence.'

'Heather Madison won't even leave the house.'

'I don't know how much more Summer can take.'

'Jon says they're the same – Heather and Summer.' We spoke quickly, not giving the other the chance to finish until in the end we both stopped and sighed.

'Summer is the last person this should happen to,' Phoenix added.

I agreed. 'Remember Arizona – how tough she came across? None of us were scared she couldn't handle the stress of coming back to the far side.'

'Summer's different. Sometimes I think it would be better if we didn't try too hard for her, just let the anniversary pass without any answers.'

'And leave her in torment!' I felt a spark of anger. 'Don't say that, Phoenix. I already talked to Summer about it. We have to solve this thing – you know we do!'

'Wait until you see her,' he warned. 'But be ready for it. And don't say I didn't prepare you.'

* * *

Phoenix stayed in the car with me until I arrived at the Madisons' place, then we exchanged our last, hurried kisses and he vanished.

'Will you be here when I come out?' I wanted to ask, but his light had fizzled and faded, and I knew I wouldn't get an answer. I walked up to the front door, trying to clear my head.

'Come in, Darina.' Jon opened the door before I knocked. 'I heard your car. For a second back there I thought you had someone with you.'

'No, I'm alone.' A breath of air blew from behind – a cold, creepy reminder for Phoenix and me to take more care in future.

Summer's dad opened the door wide. 'I told Heather you were coming. She's in her studio, looking at the pictures I shot this morning.'

Shaking off Hunter's warning signal, I glanced nervously across the hall. 'You want me to go ahead?'

He nodded. 'I'll make coffee,' he said as he disappeared into the kitchen.

So I crossed the hall and tapped on the studio door, feeling the silence in the space where there used to be music and laughter. There was no answer from inside the room but I pushed open the door anyway and was greeted by the same jumble of stacked canvases and unused paints and brushes that I'd noticed last time I was here.

Heather didn't turn or look up. She seemed engrossed in the prints laid out on a table in front of her, running her fingers lightly over their glossy surface. I noticed again how like her daughter she was, especially from behind, with the lines on her face and other marks of grief hidden. Her fair hair hung loose past her shoulders and she wore the kind of flowered top and floaty skirt that Summer liked. When she spoke, it was with the same gentle voice. 'Come look at these pictures of Hartmann,' she invited. 'See the spring flowers.'

I went and stood beside her, struggling to find something to say to fill the long silence.

'Summer loved the spring,' Heather told me. 'It was her favourite time of year. Look at the lake, how beautiful it is.'

'I was there this morning. It's pretty.'

'It's over a year now,' she sighed, still stroking the pictures with her fingertips. 'Since Arizona drowned, I mean.'

I shook my head in confusion and for the first time Heather glanced up.

'You thought I meant my daughter?'

'No. I mean, I knew you couldn't be talking about Summer . . .' I trailed off.

'I think about Arizona a lot,' Heather confessed. 'And Jonas and Phoenix – all of them. We families, we're all so different, but we have the one terrible thing in common. And their friends too – you share what we feel.' She paused then and gazed out of the large window overlooking the mountains. Then, without saying anything, she led me from the studio to Summer's room.

I steeled myself not to give way to sadness, to try and be some kind of support to this woman who had lost her child.

'You know how it feels?' she asked suddenly, standing by her daughter's bed looking at more photographs – this time of Summer playing her guitar. There were close-ups of a cloud of golden hair, a glimpse of pale skin, a curve of lips. And there were distant shots of Summer playing a concert, surrounded by bright lights, then behind the scenes: of her joking with me on two of the shots; one of her talking sound levels with Ezra and Parker, who were dressed in their trademark black T-shirts; another of her laughing with Jordan and Logan. It was how we used to be – happy.

'It feels like we're all being smothered,' Heather told me. 'All of us, under a blanket of sorrow and there's no way out.'

'Do you talk to anyone?' I asked quietly, thinking of

Kim in her sun-filled office, amazed that I was standing here recommending a shrink to Heather Madison. 'It might help.'

'Nothing helps,' came the heavy, dull answer. 'Except being with people who know what I'm going through, but without having to speak about it. Then it eases for a while.'

I heard Jon's footsteps in the hall, heading for the studio. He heard our voices and changed direction, bringing cups of coffee on a tray.

'Jon thinks I should start to paint,' Heather told me as he put the tray on Summer's bedside table. 'But I don't have the motivation.'

'He's right.' Painting beautiful landscapes was better than being smothered, better than going down under the weight of the past. 'Don't you ever think it's what Summer would want?'

Heather flinched at my words. 'That's what people say,' she said, struggling to keep her voice steady. 'They say you should let go, move on – all those shallow phrases, but they don't know.'

Standing by the window, Jon shook his head. 'Honey, Darina's trying to help.'

'Move on – what does that mean?' she asked me.

'I didn't say that exactly. I know it's not easy.'

127

'Does it mean I should let go? They expect me to turn my back on all those beautiful memories, to forget the most wonderful part of my life, my reason for living?'

'It's OK,' Jon soothed, going to her and putting his arms around her.

She buried her face in his shoulder and her words came out muffled and faint. 'I'm not moving anywhere. I can't take a single step out of this hell until they find my daughter's killer,' she sobbed.

7

I took on board Heather's message loud and clear and translated it into: *Darina, girl, get it together, solve this thing!*

If I'd listened earlier to Phoenix's doubts about continuing, I came away from the Madisons' house knowing that I would push as hard as I could to knit together the strands of evidence to form the right pattern – no holes, loose ends or dropped stitches. As I drove home, I reminded myself that I only had twelve days left.

Do it! I told myself again.

The hard fact was, I reminded myself, that Summer's case was different to Jonas and Arizona. Back then I'd been pretty certain from the start that the answers were local. Example: I learned early on that Jonas had a love rival in Matt Fortune, a kid who lived in Ellerton and went to the same school. The question was how to link him with Jonas's accident. And again, Arizona worked hard to hide it, but once I learned some vital facts about her relationship with Kyle Keppler – that he dated Arizona but had a fiancée over in Forest Lake – a clear theory about why she drowned in Hartmann came through.

Not this time. However many times I ran through events leading up to Summer's death, which I did as I lay in bed that night, the story spread out across the map, as far away and as random as Venice, Florida and Pennington, New Jersey.

I got up next morning feeling wrecked, stood under the shower, got dressed and went downstairs in a daze.

'You just missed Hannah,' Laura informed me, 'I told her you were in the shower.'

'Jeez!' Glancing through the window, I saw Hannah getting back into her car. I ran outside and caught her before she pulled away from the kerb.

'Hey, Darina.' Hannah was another person who looked like she hadn't slept. Her fair hair was mussed and flyaway; there were dark circles under her eyes. 'I wasn't sure you'd be in school today,' she said.

'I'll be there around midday for the rehearsal. I have to see someone first.'

'Cool. I guess it can wait.' She pushed the lever into Drive.

'Really? Five minutes back you thought whatever it is was important enough to detour down my street and knock on my door.'

'Yeah, but maybe I'm being crazy.'

For once, Hannah didn't seem sure of herself, so I slid into the car beside her. 'Go ahead – share,' I insisted.

'So tell me if I'm being weird, OK.'

'Speak, Hannah!'

'You remember that guy on Summer's site, the one who got mad because he couldn't buy a ticket?'

'JakB.' Who could forget his neon skull icon and his sick messages?

'He showed up on my doorstep.'

My jaw fell open. 'When? How?'

'Last night. Don't ask me how he figured out where I lived, but there he was, hammering on my door telling me he wouldn't leave until I gave him entry to the concert.'

'What part of "no" does this guy not understand?' I wanted to know. 'So what was he like, this JakB?'

'Creepy. Pale, like he never goes out in the daylight. He has long, greasy hair.'

'Don't tell me – he's skinny and he wears a black T-shirt with a goth motif.'

'An exploding skull with a bullet hole,' Hannah shuddered. 'And if he reached out and touched you, his hands would be clammy. You know the type.'

'You told him no?' I checked. 'The tickets are sold out, period.'

'I told him. But he said he already knew it and he was here for a backstage pass, a job on security – anything that would get him into the concert.'

'You told him no,' I said again through gritted teeth. The guy was harder to get rid of than a rash.

'That's when the abuse began. I was home alone and he started practically trying to break down the door.'

'Jeez, Hannah! Did you call the cops?'

'He grabbed my phone before I could do it. He wouldn't stop yelling how he was Summer's biggest fan and anyway *she* wants him at her concert.'

'Oh no,' I groaned. I wanted to block my ears and not hear the rest.

'*She*, Summer wants him there!' Hannah repeated. 'JakB talks to her, Darina. He believes he has communication with her from beyond the grave.'

I calmed Hannah down and told her no way was she overreacting. JakB was one scary, crazy kid and she should drive straight to school and inform Miss Jones about what had happened. 'Show her the comments on the website, say that he tried to force entry into your house – tell her to hand the whole thing over to the principal and then you stay out of it, you hear?'

'Or we could ignore it,' she suggested, still doubtful.

'Hand it over,' I insisted. 'By the way, you didn't give Crazy Guy his backstage pass, did you?'

She stared at me with some of her old fiery energy. 'You think I'm nuts?' she said as she drove away.

I called after her that I would see her at rehearsal and check that she'd done what I'd said.

But right now I had an appointment with the deputy sheriff.

'Hello, Darina. You look like you didn't get much sleep,' he told me when I walked into his office.

'People always tell me that,' I grunted. 'It's great for my self-esteem.'

'Sit. Do you drink coffee? Or Coca-Cola?'

'Neither, thanks.' It was my first time in a sheriff's office and I sat awkwardly across the desk from Henry Jardine, taking in the framed diplomas on the wall and the family photograph – of him, wife and two kids – propped against his computer.

'So how did you know Dean Dawson?' he asked, sifting through some paperwork on his desk.

'Not me exactly. It was more my stepdad actually.'

'Yeah – your stepdad, Jim Wright. I know him.'

Small town! And it seemed Jardine's total recall had kicked back in. Or maybe he'd checked me out before I arrived, read the file on me as one of the chief witnesses to the Summer shooting and put all the pieces into place.

'Dean was the kind you can't afford to lose – good cop, all-round good guy. He'd still be working on the Madison case if he was around.'

Thanks for the smooth lead in, I thought. 'I visited with Summer's mom and dad yesterday,' I told him. 'It's so sad.'

'I plan to pay them a visit myself,' Jardine said, slipping the papers into a transparent plastic file. The deputy sheriff obviously liked a tidy desk.

'To talk about the possible Fichtner link?' I asked eagerly.

'You don't let that one go, do you?' he smiled.

I sat frowning on the edge of my seat, thinking *Don't patronize me!*

Jardine recognized the resentment in my expression and reined in the smile. 'Something else came up, something you might like to think about, linked in a roundabout way to your buddy Zak Rohr.'

Zak? How did we get there?

'Zak has an older brother, right?'

'Brandon.'

'Brandon keeps bad company, just like Zak. And while I agree with you that Zak was more or less there for the ride when Miller and Stafford burned down the janitor's store, I can't say the same for his big brother.'

'So you won't charge Zak?' I asked. Any scrap of good news was worth clinging on to.

'Not this time,' Jardine agreed. 'But focus on his big brother for a second. Brandon is in with a bad crowd – we both know that for sure. He has a particular buddy named Oscar Thorne, currently in detention at a Denver correctional facility for a drugs deal gone wrong. Thorne wasn't the main mover in the operation, but he was in deep enough to get a two-year sentence.' Jardine noticed I was having trouble following his thread. 'Listen. These drugs people crawl over this town like any other. They deal on street corners, in the leisure centres, down the shopping mall, sometimes in broad daylight. And there are times when things turn nasty then the guns and knives come out.'

I was starting to nod, beginning to make connections.

'Now we get to April thirtieth last year,' Jardine went on. 'We put a cordon around the mall within ten minutes of the shooting, and guess who was in Starbucks drinking coffee at the same time as you?'

'Oscar Thorne?' I guessed.

135

'Right. We searched him for drugs but for once he was clean. However, we did learn something interesting. Under questioning, Thorne admitted he was a marked man. He'd screwed up a big deal the previous week and now the main guys, the importers, were gunning for him.'

'But,' I argued before Jardine could get to the end of his account, 'the guy who shot Summer wasn't a drug dealer, he was a psycho, shooting at random . . .'

'Listen,' he said again. 'Try this – the drugs boss sends a hit man after Thorne. Hit man tracks Thorne down to the mall, spots his target drinking coffee, takes aim from twenty metres, gets ready to pull the trigger.'

'And suddenly Summer walks into his line of fire,' I gasped.

'Civilian casualty,' Jardine said. 'Collateral damage in the international drugs war.'

I needed to see Brandon to ask him about Oscar Thorne.

Jardine had been clever, I realized. He'd let me in on the insider information because he wanted to make use of my link with Brandon. 'I want you to ask him about Thorne,' he'd told me. 'And come back to me with any new facts – got it?'

What could I do? I had to agree.

136

But the first thing I did after leaving Jardine's office was to drive to school. It was ten minutes before noon and I headed for the theatre round the back of the main block.

Something was happening in the entrance – a small group had gathered, a couple of guys were fighting. As I got nearer I saw it was Logan and someone else. The second kid wore a black T-shirt. He had his back to me and I couldn't make him out.

'What happened?' I asked Christian Oldman, who was standing next to Parker Simons.

In the middle of the action, Logan socked his opponent on the jaw. The other kid landed face up, flat on the ground. I looked down at his short, straw-coloured hair and his shades lying beside him on the ground. It was Ezra Powell.

'Logan went crazy,' Parker cut in. 'Ezra was supposed to be discussing sound levels for his solo with him. He must have said something bad. Logan hit out.'

'That's so not like Logan,' I muttered. We were talking about Mr Sensible, remember.

Ezra was down and Logan was on top of him, raising his fist to hit again. Seeing that Logan was about to land himself in big trouble, Christian stepped in, grabbing Logan's raised arm and wrenching hard so that Logan toppled backwards. This gave Ezra time to get on to his knees and let Parker step in to help him to his feet. On the way up, Ezra grabbed his shades and put them back on to cover the strawberry birthmark under his left eye. I knew he was self-conscious about the mark and wasn't surprised that he seemed more focused on concealing this than the fact that he'd been socked on the jaw by Logan.

'Fight's over!' Christian told Logan, keeping hold of his right arm. Christian is a county-level junior boxing champion, by the way.

By this time Jordan came running. 'Logan, what in God's name did he say to you?' she demanded, getting in between Christian and Logan. She saw me and drew me in. 'Logan totally lost it back there.'

'Let go of me,' Logan told Christian, who eased his grip but kept a warning hold.

'What did Ezra say?' Jordan wanted to know. Like me, she'd never seen Logan lose his cool before.

'Nothing. Something about Darina. He's a loser. Nothing!'

'Something about me?' I demanded.

'That's all you're going to get,' Christian advised, finally deciding that it was safe to let Logan loose because by this time Parker had led Ezra away to a safe distance. 'Ezra wound Logan up is all.'

'Fight over,' Lucas Hart confirmed. 'Time to get back to rehearsal.'

As people drifted into the auditorium, Jordan and I grabbed a moment with Logan, who was still breathing hard. 'So?' Jordan demanded.

'Come on, Logan, what did Ezra say about me?' We sandwiched him and held him back in the doorway.

'Ezra's a dumb idiot,' he muttered.

'Er, excuse me!' Jordan shook her head. 'Ezra Powell may be a geek and a wimp, but no way is he dumb.'

'He has brains coming out of his ears,' I agreed.

'So he came across with the know-it-all routine. "Do the solo this way, not your way. Your way sucks!"'

'I thought it was me he insulted?' I spread my hands, palms upwards.

'So why hit him?' Jordan still wanted to know.

'He stepped over a line,' was all Logan would give us, rubbing his knuckles where they had begun to hurt. 'I guess I'm stressed out,' he muttered. 'Do me a favour, you two. Drop it.'

After this, it wasn't a great rehearsal. People were on edge, forgetting lyrics and missing their cues. We all worried Miss Jones, who knew nothing about the fight, though she'd heard through Hannah about JakB's recent craziness.

'Maybe the situation is too hard to handle,' she confided in Hannah, her principal assistant. 'As we get near to the anniversary, emotions are bound to be running high.'

'True,' Hannah agreed. She said maybe it would be cool to finish early today and try again tomorrow.

So by three-thirty p.m. I was out of the school grounds and aiming to fulfil my ambition to have a serious talk with Brandon at his house.

I hope he's home, I thought. *And I hope Sharon is not.* My heart was beating fast as I drove down their street, glad when I saw the Harley parked in the Rohrs' drive.

Brandon heard me arrive. 'Hey, Darina,' he said in that flat tone which was hard to read. Surprised? Irritated? A little bit glad even? He stood on the porch, tapping the rail, one foot dangling over the step. 'Don't tell me – let me guess. Something went wrong with the car.'

'Yeah, whatever.' I was happy to let him think what he wanted. 'I only come calling when I need a car technician. But no – actually I want to talk about Zak.'

'What did he do now?' Brandon backed under the porch and jerked his head – an invitation for me to come into the house.

I followed him in, beating off memories of the times I used to call here to see Phoenix. The place looked the same – plain furniture, worn-out rugs, hardly any pictures or lamps. The TV was switched on with the sound down in a corner of the room.

'Zak isn't in any more trouble,' I told Brandon. 'And you'll be happy to know that he's off the hook over the fire incident. I have it from the horse's mouth.'

'Wow, Darina, you're a magician. One wave of your magic wand and it's happy ever after.'

I was ready to turn round and walk out, except Zak wasn't the real reason I was here. 'What is it with you, Brandon?' I challenged. 'Why do you always put people down?'

'It's genetic,' he said with a faint laugh, eyeing me in that way of his which suggested strongly that he wouldn't be wasting time talking to me if he hadn't made the death-bed pact with Phoenix. 'So which horse's mouth are we talking about exactly?'

'A cop down at the sheriff's office – Jardine, the one who made the arrest. He's now ready to accept Zak didn't play any part in setting the fire.'

'And he's your best buddy?' Brandon taunted.

'No, actually . . .' I began then I switched tack. 'OK, so why am I letting you get under my skin. I don't owe you anything.'

'Not even an explanation,' he agreed, turning his back to take his jacket off a hook. Then he seemed to hesitate.

'Is that the only reason you came – to tell me about the law's sudden show of leniency towards my kid brother?'

'No, there's something else.' I'd better come clean or Brandon would be zipping up his jacket and firing up the Harley. 'I need to know what you can tell me about Oscar Thorne.'

Brandon stopped mid-zipper. He came up to me real close. 'Don't even go there,' he warned.

I tried hard not to give in to his angry stare. 'Your buddy Oscar was in the mall when Summer got shot. Now he's in jail. I know that much.'

'*He* was there, but I wasn't,' Brandon said even more fiercely. 'End of story.'

'The cops are looking at a drugs link.' I would say the rest of this even if he knocked me down and stepped right over me. 'There's a chance that Summer walked into a bullet that was meant for your buddy. What do you think?'

Brandon took hold of both my arms and walked me backwards towards the door. 'I'm not listening. If you know what's good for you, you're not asking. You're not even thinking. And you're out of here.'

It was true – he'd pushed me out of the door on to the porch and sent me stumbling down the step.

Back in the car, still shaking, I had the radio tuned to a

news station as I turned the ignition. A female voice was announcing breaking headline news. '*Police investigating the fatal shooting of two students in Venice, Florida have made an arrest in Brooklyn earlier today. This comes after months of close cooperation between state authorities across America, including the authorities in New Jersey. Police in New York State say that the suspect may be involved in a total of five separate shooting sprees. They have named him as Scott Fichtner, a twenty-year-old ex-music student and currently unemployed white male.*'

I'd been talking to myself a lot lately, and now was no exception.

'Phoenix, are you around? Is anybody listening to me, because I have important things to say!'

I drove away from the Rohrs' house and found myself going in aimless circles, getting closer and closer to Centennial and the freeway out past Turkey Shoot Ridge. I drove round one block maybe five or six times, trying to resist the temptation.

'Do you hear me?' I yelled through the open top of my car. Where were the Beautiful Dead when I most needed them? 'They arrested Fichtner. He's an ex-music student. How creepy is that?'

'Not so loud, Darina,' a voice next to me said. I didn't need to turn to look to know it was the overlord himself.

143

'They arrested Fichtner for the two shootings,' I repeated. 'They already linked him with at least three others.'

Hunter sat upright, staring straight ahead. In profile, his face looked even more like a statue carved out of stone – pale, with the high, tattooed forehead and long, straight nose, his features completely immobile. 'Including Ellerton?' he asked, hardly moving his lips.

'It has to be including us,' I retorted. 'We follow the Fichtner pattern – gunman opens fire in a mall, sprays bullets around, hits whoever happens to be in the way.'

Hunter reacted by sitting in silence as I drove once more around the block.

'Where do you want me to go?' I asked. 'If you're not planning to talk to me, why did you come?'

'Park up,' he muttered, making a weary gesture of putting two fingertips to his forehead and giving it a small circular rub.

I found a side street lined with shop units that were either empty or closed for the evening, parked the car and waited.

'You've been busy,' Hunter commented at last. 'You did what Dean told you to do – that's good.'

A compliment from Hunter? A first. 'I went to see

Henry Jardine. Plus, I called in on Brandon. There's a lot to share with you.'

'Save it until we get to Foxton,' he ordered.

Cool – I'll see Phoenix! I couldn't keep the joy off my face.

'We don't want to raise any suspicions so I plan to get you back home by midnight.'

'What am I, Cinderella?' I asked. As usual, I got to go to the ball and dance with Prince Charming, but then, when the clock struck twelve, the rags and the pumpkin came back.

'I need to talk to you, Darina.' Hunter turned in his seat and gave me a long, cold stare. 'Before I take you out there, I need your cooperation.'

'Shoot,' I said, taking note of the use of the word 'cooperation' from the guy who usually used mind-bending tactics to dish out the orders. 'I'm listening.'

'I've been impressed by your work,' he went on.

Whoa, another compliment! This conversation was so not what I expected.

'But also a little worried to see you engaging with events that don't concern you.'

He means Marie and Mentone! I realized, and of course Hunter read my mind.

'Right. That topic is off limits. It has nothing to do with

Summer or Phoenix, or any of the Beautiful Dead.'

'It has to do with you,' I pointed out. 'If you're not Beautiful Dead, what are you?'

'An overlord is not here for himself, Darina. I'm here for them – the others. My history is just that – long dead, locked up in the past. Besides, there's no mystery attached. My killer was tried and convicted. He paid the penalty for his crime.'

'So you don't want to talk about the fact that Marie had a daughter and she named her Hester?' My big mouth got the better of me the way it always did. I spoke the words and watched Hunter's face change in a second from stone-cold impassive to soul in torment.

Hunter closed his eyes and tilted his head back, struggling to regain control. When he looked at me again the eyes were fired up with anger. 'What's the use?' he demanded. 'I try to explain, I lay out the boundaries as clear as day and you still overstep the mark.'

'I'm sorry. Forget I said it.'

'You don't talk about Marie – not ever! Not to others and especially not to me. I won't listen to you dirty her name!'

'I said I'm sorry.'

'Darina – one more move like this and I'm through with you. You sit there and listen, you hear? If I had the power to wipe just part of your memory I'd do it. I'd take out all your knowledge of my wife. You wouldn't even know her name.'

I felt the blade of his anger scythe me down, leave me lying flat on the ground. I held on to the sides of my seat and sat in dread.

'But that's fine tuning and it's not possible,' he went on. I can zap the whole of your Beautiful Dead memory or none of it. Which is it going to be?'

'Please, Hunter . . .' I knew that once again he was a millimetre away from tossing me out of their lives like garbage. Those eyes – they were burning into me.

'You understand your choice, Darina? Either you stick with the facts surrounding Summer's death or you leave for good. No Foxton, no Phoenix!'

I was so scared I was hardly able to nod.

'Which is it?'

'I stick with Summer,' I promised. 'I do exactly what you tell me.'

'Drive out to the aspen ridge,' Hunter told me. 'Park where no one will see the car.'

I drove fast and the overlord slouched down in the seat, facing straight ahead, assuming it was now safe to leave me to my own thoughts.

In the hour it took to drive, I went over what he'd just put me through – the anger, the threat to throw me back into the hell of everyday existence minus my memories of Phoenix and the Beautiful Dead. Did he mean it, or was it another stupid mind game?

The reason I suspected this? Hunter knew me well enough to recognize the rebel in me. He understood that ordering me *not* to do something was as good as saying, 'Go ahead, do it your way.'

Occasionally I glanced at him. His face was still turned away, his gaze was fixed on the steep rise of the darkening hillside with the neon cross in the distance, or on the small cabins lining the road at the Foxton junction. *He's playing a game, he's pushing me to find out more about Hester*, I decided. But I was still in a state of shock and not ready to put it to the test. I drove along the creek side, heading into the mountains. When we reached the end of the dirt road, I took the car fifty metres off the track across scrubland and parked it under the trees.

'Stick to the topic we agreed on,' Hunter reminded me as he stepped out of the car and slammed the door.

I shivered as I got out on the driver's side, caught in a sudden blast of icy wind blowing across the valley from Amos Peak. 'We're back to winter,' I grumbled, zipping up my denim jacket. I wasn't kidding – there were heavy clouds gathering over the jagged horizon and that arctic wind.

'Walk,' he ordered, striding ahead without looking back. He skirted the ancient water tower then dipped down the hillside, quickly disappearing from view.

I swore as I tried to keep up. Sure, Hunter was angry with me and my big mouth, but did he have to give me such a hard time? I went too fast and in my carelessness loosened some shale and went sliding out of control until I caught hold of a bush and stopped. I swore again, put my hand to my mouth and sucked a spine out of the flesh at the base of my thumb. When I looked up I saw Donna and Iceman waiting for us by the razor-wire fence.

'Where's Summer?' Hunter called down the hill. The wind whipped his voice back up the slope towards me.

'Waiting in the barn,' Donna called back. 'Dean and Phoenix are headed up to the ridge. Dean sensed intruders.'

So I don't get to see Phoenix! If my mood was bad before, it plummeted down into a deep, dark pit when I heard this news.

'Go tell them to patrol along the ridge all the way to the aspen stand, then back via Angel Rock to Government Bridge.' Hunter gave Iceman an instant order. 'And tell them not to come back until they're one hundred per cent sure there are no far-siders snooping around.'

Iceman nodded and went off, soon disappearing into the shadows that had swept down the hillside. Hunter strode on towards the barn, while Donna waited for me, her short red hair the one point of colour in the gathering dusk. 'Have you brought some news?' she asked, linking arms with me and half carrying me forward.

I felt her zombie strength sweep me on. 'Plenty,' I gasped.

'Cool. I'm – *we're* all worried about Summer. She's not doing well.'

'I know – Phoenix told me – but things are coming together,' I promised. I wanted to spin this visit out now, to make sure I was still around when Phoenix got back from patrolling the ridge. I paused to glance up at Angel Rock silhouetted on the horizon – an outcrop of granite worn by the wind and rain into the shape of a Christmas angel: head, body, wings and all.

'Walk, Darina!' Hunter repeated without turning his head.

I didn't have any choice – Donna half lifted me off my feet to catch up with him before he reached the barn.

We went inside. Once more I breathed in the musty, dusty smell of old straw and cobwebs and waited for my eyes to get used to the interior. A solitary oil lamp placed on the steps lit the dark space – not enough to define the jumble of farm tools and horse tack stacked against the walls, but enough to make out Summer's pale figure sitting halfway up the steps. Lit from below by the yellow lamp glow, she looked unreal and ghostly.

'I brought Darina,' Hunter said abruptly, turning to leave the barn and taking Donna with him. He glanced towards me, the warning look still present in those glinting, steel-grey eyes.

Slowly I crossed the barn and went up the steps to sit beside Summer. 'How are you doing?' I asked in my

151

blundering way. I mean, I could see she was totally not doing well – it was obvious from one quick glance.

Summer sat with her knees crooked, her thin arms clasping her legs, her fair hair falling about her shoulders like a cloak. Her eyes were big and dark, unblinking. I can honestly say I have never seen anyone so pale. 'I wish it was over,' she sighed.

'It will be soon.' I did a quick count – eleven days was all we had.

She turned her head towards me. 'I don't care what happens to me, Darina. I just want it to finish.'

'*I* care!' I shot back. 'I need answers for you. I *care!*'

Her eyelids fluttered and she sighed. 'I'm empty – here!' Slowly she raised her hand and touched her heart. 'I have no feelings any more, just a space.'

'Listen to me.' Gently I took her cold hand in mine. 'You don't have to do anything, OK? You let me, Hunter and the rest work it out.'

Summer looked me in the eyes. 'People get hurt,' she sighed. 'We think this is about justice, but it's also about pain and suffering. That's what I can't stand – people hurting so much.'

I couldn't argue with this, so I stayed silent.

'There's been enough already – blood, fear, and the rest.'

'But if we stop . . .' I began. JakB, Scott Fichtner, the Ellerton drugs baron – one of them walked away unpunished.

Just then an extra-strong gust of wind rattled the door handle and whistled through the gaping window frame in the loft above. Summer shuddered and closed her eyes.

I knew I couldn't convince her, but I held her hand tight, talked on in the way mothers do to kids emerging from nightmares. 'I'm almost there. You leave it to me and in another couple of days I'll have the answer. *Then* you can leave.'

She shook her head so slightly that I almost missed it. 'Do you know how it feels to have this – space?' She touched her heart again, then fluttered her fingers against her chest. 'Emptiness, where love used to be.'

'I do,' I answered softly. I was scared she was going to fade away in front of my eyes. 'After Phoenix died – believe me, I do.' The hollow where your heart should be, the dark place. 'But there's a way out, trust me.'

Somehow I was getting through to her at last. I felt her squeeze my hand and saw her raise her downcast eyes. 'So go ahead,' she whispered. 'What did you find out?'

'They arrested Fichtner. He's my main man, remember?'

Summer nodded. 'I don't know if it's him though. I

153

looked at his picture, but I didn't recall his face.'

'That's OK, your memory's smashed to pieces by the trauma. But he fits. He travels the country carrying out these random, crazy killings. The cops are investigating the copycat incidents right now.'

'Cool,' she murmured without meaning it, dipping back down into hopelessness.

'Trust me!' I said again. 'And there's more. If the Fichtner theory falls apart, there's a guy called Oscar Thorne, a lowlife drugs baron. I went to see Deputy Sheriff Jardine, Dean's buddy. He told me the Bishop County office is following a different trail that puts Thorne in the frame as the intended victim. A big drugs deal had gone bad – the dealers were ready to shoot it out between them.'

Summer nodded and I could tell she'd withdrawn back into her empty space.

'Then there's Crazy Guy number two,' I gabbled. 'Did you ever read comments on your website from a guy calling himself JakB?'

'I don't remember.'

'He uses an exploding skull's head icon. He calls himself your "number one fan".'

Summer shrugged. 'There was a heap of weird people,' she recalled. 'Most times I didn't even read their messages through before I deleted them.'

'So now he's hassling Hannah for a backstage pass.' I pressed on, trying to grab her attention by taking her other hand and turning her towards me. The lamp flame flickered in the draught caused by the howling wind. 'He claims you and he are still in touch.'

'I can tell you that's a "no",' she said with a touch of her old, dry humour.

'Exactly! And this is a death-fixated crazy guy – the skull, the comments about love being bigger than death. Give a guy like that a gun and God knows what he's capable of!'

'So don't go near him,' she advised, sounding like Phoenix and pulling her hands free before she stood up. 'Leave it to the cops – they seem to be doing OK.'

'Where are you going?' I asked, following her quickly down the steps.

'Into the house. Are you coming?'

I overtook her and tried to open the big barn door, finding that I had to push hard against the wind. Summer gave a little smile and poked the door with her finger. I tutted as it swung open. 'Sorry,' I mumbled.

'I didn't lose all my strength – not yet.' Her smile broadened and softened. 'Come on, let's go in and sit by the fire – you must be freezing.'

So we went into the cosy kitchen where a log fire

burned and a metal jug bubbled on the primitive stove. Summer poured two mugs of steaming coffee from the jug. 'I'm writing a new song,' she told me. 'Would you like to hear?'

'Do you need to ask?' Excited, I sat across the hearth from her, sipped my coffee and watched as she rested her guitar across her knees. *Just like the old days*, I thought. And I was able to sit there and fall under her spell, shutting out the fears and doubts, the ticking clock and all the crap I had to deal with in the real world.

Summer bent her head over the guitar, letting her hair swing forward. Her left hand slid up and down the frets while her right hand picked out the notes that flowed like water in the creek. And her voice – softer, more mellow than before, and the words sadder than anything you ever heard. 'I loved you so / But it was time to go / You spoke my name / I never came / 'Cos it was time for me to go.'

I was in tears before the end of the first verse. 'It's perfect,' I told her when the song ended. In my mind I carried the image of me waiting that last time for Phoenix by Deer Creek, and his voice, not Summer's, singing, 'You spoke my name / I never came . . .'

'I wrote it for my parents,' she said softly.

Delving into my jacket pocket, I pulled out a crumpled

156

slip of paper and a pen. 'Write it down,' I pleaded. 'The words and the music.'

Summer did as I asked, her hand shaking slightly. 'Give it to my mom,' she said as she handed the paper back. 'Say you didn't know you had it – you found it tucked away in a notebook.'

Nodding, I folded the paper and put it back in my pocket.

'Phoenix is here,' Summer said, suddenly getting up and going to the door, opening it to let me see him striding across the yard, lashed by wind and rain, looking wild and somehow angry. His white T-shirt and dark hair were soaked through as he came up into the porch.

'Take care, Darina,' Summer said as she left.

I ran to throw my arms around Phoenix, my heart thudding as if I was the one who had run down from the ridge. 'I heard there were intruders. Was anyone up there?'

He shook his head, resting his head on my shoulder for a moment before pulling away. 'No one. Dean was mistaken. Now let me get out of these wet clothes.'

I watched him peel off his T-shirt and fling it on to the table, then I picked up a towel from the back of a chair and laid it across his broad shoulders. 'When did it start to rain?' I asked.

'A couple of minutes back.' He towelled his hair roughly as I took in every centimetre of his smooth torso. 'What are you staring at?' he asked with his little intimate grin.

'You!' I was in his arms again and we were kissing, I was experiencing the marble coldness of his skin and, at the same time, the heat of his passion. 'What do you expect when you strip half naked in front of me?'

He kissed me again, long and hard. 'I got back here as fast as I could. I saw Hunter.'

'He's angry with me,' I confessed. 'But then, what's new? How bad is the storm? Will the Beautiful Dead have to leave?'

Phoenix shook his head. 'It's wild out there but there's no thunder and lightning, no electrical stuff.'

So no danger to their supernatural powers. Phoenix and the others could stay on the far side and ride out the wind and rain.

'Maybe I can stay with you until the storm blows over?' I suggested.

'Don't get up your hopes,' he replied, running his fingers over my face and down my neck to the hollow at the base of my throat. 'Isn't Hunter planning to get you back home before midnight?'

'How did you know . . . oh, OK, you read his mind.

That's why you looked mad. But I'll tell him he can't send me home in this.'

'Actually, he can.' Hunter himself had flung open the door and found us locked together. Our passionate embrace obviously left him unmoved. 'You had your time with Summer, Darina. Now it's time to leave.'

'I don't believe you!' I groaned. I could see Hunter over Phoenix's shoulder, a lock of long grey hair whipped across his cheek by the wind, his eyes fixed on me.

'Summer doesn't agree that Fichtner is your man.' As Hunter came into the room, he must have given Phoenix the silent order to step back from me. I felt Phoenix's body stiffen as he released me. 'How about you, Darina? Do you stick with your serial-killer scenario?'

'I do.' Briefly I wished that Phoenix would stand up to the overlord, just once. Couldn't he resist the order, even for a second?

Phoenix caught my thought and quickly looked down at the rug in embarrassment.

'I'm sorry – I know how it is,' I whispered.

He looked up and put on a smile for me, glanced towards Hunter and took another silent instruction to leave the room.

I planned to protest, but Hunter zapped that thought away. Instead I sat down by the fire in a resentful slouch.

159

'I want you to go home and get some sleep,' he told me. 'You need to be up early, to follow up the alternative JakB theory.'

This focused my still-wandering mind and I waited for more.

'You saw Summer's killer?'

'From under a baseball cap,' I reminded him. 'And he was wearing aviator shades.'

'So you need to take a look at JakB. Is he too tall, too short, too heavy, too skinny?'

This made sense. 'You're right. He's been hassling Hannah, not taking no for an answer. I expect he'll show up again soon.'

'Why not throw him some bait? Reply to him on Summer's website, tell him you can get him a concert ticket.'

'Fix up a meeting?'

'Take a look at him from a distance. No need to get too close.'

'OK.'

'Meanwhile, stay in touch with Jardine and let him check out the Oscar Thorne deal.'

'You reckon it's too dangerous for me?' Foolishly I imagined that Hunter was looking out for me in warning me away from the underbelly of Ellerton society.

He laughed. 'I mean, let the cops do the work because they have a network of contacts, something solid to go on. Let them go ahead and interview Thorne in his prison cell.'

'Doh!' I pretended to beat my forehead with the flat of my palm. *Dummy, Darina, for thinking that Hunter cared!*

'Now go,' the overlord instructed, opening the door again and waiting for me to leave.

Unbelievable! Hunter had forced me out on to the hillside in the worst storm this spring. Rain lashed down from the night sky, driving against me as I battled towards the ridge. My denim jacket was no protection and I was soon soaked to the skin.

Phoenix, for pity's sake, lend me a hand! Somebody, help!

The more I leaned into the wind and rain, the stronger it seemed to grow. Water was rushing down the slope in rivulets, dragging loose pebbles with it. A gust of wind tore up a sapling and sent it crashing against the trunk of an older, sturdier tree. I thought I would never make it to the water tower, and when I did I found that the whole ancient, rusty structure creaked and swayed so much that I dare not take shelter. Instead, I stumbled on.

This will teach you a lesson! I told myself. *In future, even if you suspect Hunter's playing mind games, don't ever think about defying Hunter over the Marie and Hester thing!*

It was pitch black, the heavens had opened, the wind was savage. I'd be lucky not to catch my death of cold.

I was under the stand of aspens, about thirty metres from my car when I spotted the other vehicle parked by the trees I usually used for cover. It was a small car, a Honda like the one Logan drove. I would hardly have seen it except that it was white. The wind tore through the leaves overhead, ripping into me with the force of a tornado. A branch snapped and fell to the ground, just missing the Honda.

Now I was divided – should I get in my car and drive the hell out, or should I check out the mystery vehicle? And how had Phoenix and Dean missed it when they were out on patrol? Did it mean that it had just arrived? If so, where was the driver?

Check it out, I told myself, my heart in my mouth and searching for an explanation of why I was here in case it turned out that I needed one. I went unwillingly, I can tell you.

I got close to the white car, close enough to squint through the dark and check the registration plate. *Logan's number!*

I stood trying to absorb this fact. Logan's car was parked at the end of the Foxton track where no one except me and a few hunters ever came. It was night-time, the middle of a bad storm. Everything led to the conclusion that he'd followed me here.

And I thought you were over me, I said out loud in a burst of anger. *We agreed I could never look at you that way.*

Way back in the past, when I was looking for answers for Jonas, Logan and I had had this talk:

Him: I love you, Darina.

Me: But I love Phoenix.

Him: Phoenix is dead.

Me: I still love him. I'll love him for ever.

It broke Logan's heart for a while, but eventually I thought he accepted the way it was. Lately he was even dating Jordan, wasn't he?

But this was definitely Logan's car, no doubt about it. And it was empty. I opened the driver's door to make certain, felt the wind almost rip it off its hinges before I managed to force it shut again. The rain hammered on the hood and ran in torrents from under the wheel arches.

So he'd followed me and Hunter. Maybe he'd been driving through Centennial at the point just after Hunter showed up, seen him sitting next to me, giving me a hard time over my unwelcome curiosity. And Logan had wondered who the hell Hunter was and what he wanted.

It would be typical of Logan to follow at a distance in case I needed him.

But where was he now? I raised my voice to bring him back to his car. 'Logan, where are you?'

There was no answer, only the wind howling through the aspens, the rain drumming on to the roof and the hood.

And then another thought struck me. Was Logan the intruder Dean had heard?

No way. Phoenix said they didn't find any far-siders.

Maybe they did and he was lying. Anyway, maybe they set up the barrier, the force field to keep them out, just in case. Had Logan got caught up in that by mistake?

I felt my stomach wrench into knots as I left the car and staggered past the rock towards the top of the ridge. 'Logan, it's me, Darina!'

I was sure that was what had happened – the Beautiful Dead had thrown the beating wings and skulls at Logan, sent him crazy, zapped his memory clean and abandoned him to the storm. And it was my fault.

I reached a rocky ledge in the pouring rain, clung to a tree trunk as a blast of wind wrenched me off my feet. I watched as, twenty metres behind me, the same blast rocked Logan's car from side to side.

I'm out of here! A new thought struck me that I should

leave while I could. What reasons could I give Logan if he found me out here? Surely it was better to leave his memory of the whole incident zombie-wiped and let him find his own way home. But I couldn't do it – he might be in danger and I couldn't desert him. So I held on to the tree and yelled his name.

I was closer to him than I knew. I just needed to glance down ten metres to the foot of the ledge to see a body slumped against a boulder.

At first I thought it was garbage – a tent ripped up by the wind and tossed against the rock, a piece of tarpaulin from the back of a hunter's truck. But no, I knew I was fooling myself. 'Logan?' I whispered as I clambered down the slope. I reached his side and bent over him, lifting his jacket collar clear of his face.

His eyes were open but I knew he was seriously hurt. 'Don't try to move,' I whispered.

He closed his eyes, opened them again, as if he was checking that he wasn't hallucinating.

'It's OK.' I knew it wasn't, even though there was no sign of blood. 'I'm here.'

'The wind,' he murmured.

'I know. You're OK. Don't move.' I knew he couldn't.

He lay on his back in the rain, looking up at me. 'The wind.'

'I know – it pushed you over the edge. Don't worry, I'll get you out of here.'

'Or maybe I was pushed.' He said this so faintly I thought I'd imagined it. Then he sighed and closed his eyes.

'Logan, stay awake! We're going to get out, you hear!'

His eyes flickered open. 'The wind,' he whispered again.

'That's right. It's a bad storm.' He looked so weak that I felt his neck for a pulse then leaned down to listen to his breathing.

He whispered in my ear. 'Darina, I never wanted anyone except you.'

Donna and Iceman came to help me get Logan to my car. They didn't speak as they appeared in their halos of silver light, they just made me stand to one side and lifted him as if he weighed no more than a feather. They kept him flat on his back and carried him on their shoulders, letting his arms hang down. He groaned as they set him down in the car.

'Drive,' Iceman told me before he zapped Logan's mind clear of the last few minutes. Then he closed the door and he and Donna dematerialized into the darkness.

Panic squeezed my heart. Logan lay slumped beside me, his head fallen back against the hooped metal rest, his eyes almost closed. I turned on the ignition and the wipers, reversed from under the trees, hearing the tyres crunch on the shale as I swung round to face the dirt road. 'Hang on, Logan,' I pleaded. 'Talk to me. Stay awake.'

'What did I do?'

'You didn't do anything. You got caught in a storm, you fell.' I was on the track, trying to avoid the ruts and hollows. I had to get Logan to a doctor. He had to keep his eyes open. 'What were you doing here?' I asked.

'I was out at Foxton with Lucas and some other guys. I saw you drive by.'

'And you had to follow me!' I cried.

My car hit a ridge, we rattled and rolled down the next stretch, but the necklace of Foxton lights came into view, and I told Logan we were almost on the highway. 'Hang on,' I pleaded. I would break any limit, drive through any red light to get him to the hospital.

Up ahead, the spray from passing trucks rose in clouds, caught in my headlights as I waited for a gap in the traffic. The yellow indicator light flashed on-off, on-off, lighting up Logan's face and throwing it back into darkness.

He'd lost consciousness by the time we reached the hospital. His head had tilted towards me, his eyes were closed.

The paramedics came and took him out of the car. They stretchered him into the ER, hooked him up to machines, ran the first tests.

'He's going to be OK,' I told a nurse under the bright lights.

He nodded. 'You see the woman at the desk? Go talk to her. We'll take good care of your buddy.'

They needed to know Logan's name, she told me. How old was he? Where did his parents live?

I could see Logan through a glass partition. He lay under a green sheet, surrounded by machines and medics. Then they rolled screens around him.

'Logan Lavelle,' I told her. 'No mother, only a father. They live on West Seventy-Ninth, it's the street next to mine.'

Logan's dad came to the hospital at two a.m. He'd been drinking at Mike Hamill's house until the small hours, had arrived home to an urgent message that he should call the hospital. By the time I saw him in the corridor outside Logan's room, he was halfway sober.

'Mr Lavelle, my name is David Hoffmann. I'm taking care of Logan.' The doctor rested a hand on his shoulder and led him down the corridor. 'Your boy sustained a serious head injury in a fall. The scan shows damage to the skull and some pressure on the frontal lobe of the brain . . .'

I sat there feeling sick in my stomach, trying to control my breathing. The lights seemed too bright, the floor too shiny. I put my hand to my eyes and covered them, until I heard the doctor come back with Logan's dad.

'We'll do everything we can,' he promised.

'When can I see him?' Byron Lavelle asked.

'We're running a scan. I'll fetch you when we're through.'

As the doctor disappeared down the corridor, Logan's dad sat heavily beside me. He was dressed in his work clothes, with two days' stubble on his chin. I noticed that the pointed Western boots he always wore were dusty and scuffed. I closed my eyes with a feeling of total hopelessness.

We got through to four-thirty a.m. By now Laura and Jim were both at the hospital with me. Jim had taken Logan's dad to a family room on the sixth floor while Laura sat and held my hand in the corridor. 'This is because of me,' I told her.

She put her hand up to stop me. 'Don't talk. Save it for later.'

The hospital had already told us that they planned

surgery the next day. 'We have a tube in there to drain fluid from inside the skull and ease the pressure. The scan shows a blood clot. He's on anti-coagulant medication. We hope the surgery will remove the clot altogether.'

'And if it doesn't?' Byron Lavelle had asked.

Dr Hoffmann had tilted his head to one side then shrugged.

'Logan drove through the storm after me,' I said to Laura. 'He was scared I was driving into trouble.'

'That's Logan,' she sighed. 'Always looking out for you.'

'He told me he never wanted anyone except me. Word for word, that's what he said.'

Laura stared straight ahead, her face drained of colour. She didn't ask me the obvious question, which was why was I out at Foxton in the first place? She didn't say, 'Poor Logan.' She didn't say anything.

The thing was, Phoenix had lied to me. He'd told me they hadn't found any far-siders up on the ridge while all the time Logan had been there, searching for me. That was why he and Dean had set up the winged barrier. But Phoenix hadn't given me those facts.

I sat in the hospital corridor, unable to erase the picture from my mind – Logan getting out of his car, leaving the shelter of the aspens and staggering onto the ridge. Logan battered by the wind and rain, and then the Beautiful Dead wings, followed by skulls crowding in on him, terror ripping into his brain. He would put up his hands and crouch down to protect himself, he would lose his balance and fall over a sheer drop. It would feel like someone had pushed him.

The fall – a mighty blast from behind, a moment of shock then everything in slow motion . . . the tipping forward into black emptiness, the drop into thin air.

'Come home,' Laura pleaded with me. It was Tuesday midday. Logan's surgery was due to start at one-thirty p.m.

'I want to stay here.'

'Listen to your mom,' Dr Hoffmann advised. He was a young guy just out of med school – nervous, a little out of his depth. 'Go home and rest up. Logan will be in theatre all afternoon.'

'I'll be here anyway,' Byron muttered.

They took him off to the family room again where he could wait in peace.

'Come home, Darina.' Mom was begging me. 'You can be back here when Logan comes round from the anaesthetic.'

I looked up at Hoffmann. 'Can I see him before I leave?'

He nodded and showed me into Logan's room, which was full of monitors flashing numbers and graphs that showed heartbeat, pulse rate, blood pressure, whatever.

Logan lay on the bed, eyes closed, with an oxygen mask over his mouth and nose. More tubes fed into his arm, plus they'd positioned stickers and wires over his heart.

'Logan?' I crept to the bedside and leaned over him.

'Go ahead.' The doctor encouraged me to speak. 'There's a chance he can hear you even though he's in a coma. But don't expect any response.' He left me alone with the patient.

'Hey,' I breathed. 'How are you doing? . . . They're taking good care of you . . . You're going to come through this . . .'

The machines beeped and flickered their vital messages across the screens. Logan lay totally still, his face drained of colour, his thick brown hair combed back from his forehead. I touched his cheek. 'Stay with us, Logan,' I whispered. 'I need you, you hear?'

He died anyway – my Logan. My poor Logan died in the cold, dark night trying to help me. I couldn't get my head around the fact that he was dead and I was alive – Logan, who should have had a whole happy, wonderful life ahead of him.

I pictured him sitting on his porch telling me a funny story, asking me about my day. There was the Logan grin, the kind eyes that never lied – gone for ever.

My Logan died.

I got up from the kitchen table and left the house, I walked down the street to Logan's place and sat on the porch step. Any moment now he would turn the corner in his white Honda.

I watched the guy from two doors down drive his Toyota truck on to the sidewalk. I saw kids walk home from school. Late in the afternoon Byron drew up at the kerbside. He saw me on the porch step but walked right past me into the house. After five minutes I heard the faint, pressurized fizz of a beer can being opened.

Before it grew dark, Jim came to fetch me home.

The world went on, I guess. I stayed in my room.

I spoke to Phoenix, wherever he was. *You didn't tell me the truth. How can I ever trust you again?*

I knew in my heart that I had done a terrible thing. I had caused Logan to die.

Hannah and Jordan called at the house.

I stayed in my room.

I didn't want to see them. Christian texted the news that Logan's funeral was fixed for Wednesday the twenty-seventh.

'It's been three whole days.' On the Friday after Logan died Laura knocked on my door and came in. 'You need to start to make an effort – take a shower, get dressed.'

It felt like she was talking to me through a screen of clingfilm, opening her mouth to speak but not making any sense. I'd lost touch with time, with everyone around me and most of all with the Beautiful Dead.

'Today is your session with Kim Reiss,' Laura reminded me, already knowing that I wouldn't keep the appointment.

'How come the surgeons messed up?' I asked her. 'If they'd done their job, Logan would still be here.'

'Honey . . .' she began then trailed off with a sigh. 'Here's a fresh towel. I'll turn on your shower.'

I took the shower on auto-pilot, changed into clean jeans and T-shirt, caught sight of myself and turned my mirror to the wall. When I went to the window to raise the blind, a face was staring in at me.

I gasped and stepped back. For the first time in seventy-two hours I escaped the net of the past and had a reaction to a real-time event.

The guy had staring eyes. His lips were mouthing words at me through the glass. He rattled his fist against it until I thought it would shatter.

I went and opened the window – first floor, remember. Staring-guy had stood on the roof of his car and used my window ledge to haul himself up. He'd grazed the knuckles of his left hand doing it. 'What the—'

'Listen to me,' he hissed. 'You have to do something for me.'

The idea of prising the fingers of his bleeding hand away from the ledge entered my mind. I didn't care that he would drop four metres to the ground. Then I noticed something else about him – namely his black T-shirt with the exploding skull motif.

'I need to get into Summer's concert,' he snake-hissed – *S-S-Summer's cons-s-sert.*

Jeez, I went for the guy's fingers big time. 'Get the hell out!' I yelled. 'Jim, Laura, come quick!'

I couldn't make anyone hear and JakB hung on. I stared at his twisted face – the too-close-together, pale-lashed eyes and long nose, the big Adam's apple jerking up and down as he fought to cling to the ledge.

'I'll blow my brains out if I don't get a ticket,' he threatened.

Go right ahead, weirdo! Right now I had no softer side for him to appeal to. I raised my bare foot and stomped on his fingers.

'Summer means everything to me!' he grunted. He'd let go with one hand but still hung on with the other. 'She needs me there with her!'

I stamped down hard on hand number two, heard him

let out a phlegm-thickened cry as he fell, then the thud of his body against his car roof. Leaning out, I watched him slither to the sidewalk. He looked up in agony, holding his wrist and pleading with me to join him, but the last thing on my mind was running downstairs to continue my conversation with Summer Madison's 'number one fan'.

Next day, Saturday, Lucas came to the house in person and Jim let him in. The message was he wouldn't leave until I came downstairs to talk.

I wasn't ready, but Lucas sat it out, even after Jim drove to the supermarket. Hearing Logan's friend beat out a rhythm on the kitchen table drew me down in the end.

Lucas had known Logan as long as I had. He was the one in the gang we kidded along with and sometimes made fun of, especially when he grew tall and gangly and seemed never to know where to put himself without knocking something over or banging into stuff. Plus, because he didn't know how to dress other than in sloppy T-shirt and faded jeans, Lucas was not considered sexy or cool. In other words, I really liked the guy.

And I was shocked when I saw him sitting at the table, tapping his fingers. He looked like he'd been crying and was about to start again. I went and sat down by his side.

'Say it didn't happen,' he begged.

I closed my eyes and took a deep breath.

'Darina, it did *not* happen.'

'It did,' I whispered.

'When you found him – how did he look?'

'He was awake. I told him he was going to be OK.'

Lucas swallowed hard. 'Was he in pain?'

'I don't think so.'

'I told him a couple of times not to leave, but he wouldn't listen.'

No, this is too hard. The memory net was closing round me, pulling me back in.

'He saw you drive by in the storm so he set out after you. A big bunch of us – Christian, Parker, Ezra, a few others – were hanging out in Christian's dad's cabin, waiting for the rain to stop. I said, "Stay here, dude," but he set off after you.'

'I know. Believe me, I couldn't feel worse than I already do.'

Lucas stared at me for a while. 'I do believe you, Darina. But Logan wouldn't want that. One of the reasons I came here was to say no way would he have blamed you.'

'Thanks, Lucas.' Clumsy, clunky Lucas was the one trying to rescue me from myself. I reached out to stop his fingers from drumming, then held on to his hand.

He grasped my hand back, his long fingers wrapping

tight around mine. 'The funeral's Wednesday.'

'I know.'

'Logan's dad has asked the guys to carry the casket. He wants the girls to play guitar and sing songs.'

'Who's organizing the music?'

'Hannah and Jordan. They asked me to ask you . . .'

'To sing?'

He nodded. 'Yeah, Logan would love for that to happen.'

'I'll be there,' I promised.

And we both cried in my kitchen until Jim came home with the groceries.

The song I rehearsed for Logan's funeral service was Summer's new song, 'Time to Go'.

I pulled the slip of paper out of my jacket pocket, unfolded it and flattened out the creases. The words were perfect for the occasion: 'There's a hill / I'll wait until / The stars appear / And the sky grows clear / Then it's time for me to go.' And the chorus: 'I loved you so / But it was time to go / You spoke my name / I never came / 'Cos it was time for me to go.'

I sang and played softly until my voice grew into the sounds and my fingers stopped fumbling with the notes. I practised all through Saturday night and the whole of

Sunday, ready to go into school on the Monday to perform it for Hannah and Jordan.

It was only the song that got me out of the house at last. I stepped on to the porch and the spring sun dazzled me so much that I had to put on my shades. I turned left out of the drive to avoid Logan's block and made myself focus on getting to school for the midday rehearsal. I parked in the grounds next to Lucas's black SUV.

Inside the building, I avoided eye contact with students and teachers, who greeted me with sympathetic smiles. Everyone knew it had been me that found Logan on Foxton Ridge, but nobody except Lucas and the gang who were at the cabin knew the details. I walked through the main block into the theatre.

Jordan spotted me at the top of the raked auditorium. I waited as she climbed the wide steps. 'Are you OK?' she asked.

'No. But thanks for talking to me.' I was more than ready to take the blame from the girl who'd been dating the boy I'd led to his death.

Jordan sighed. 'We've been using Summer's music to get us through this,' she explained as she led me down past rows of hinged seats. 'You wouldn't believe it but we're almost ready for the concert already – five days ahead of schedule.'

I stopped her beside Row D. 'Will you sing at the funeral?' I asked.

She shook her head. 'Logan was your buddy,' she told me. 'We dated, but I always knew he belonged to you.'

'Sing anyway.' I took out the 'Time to Go' music and showed it to her. 'It's a new song by Summer. I found it between some other sheets of music when I visited the Madisons' house.'

Jordan took the paper. She chewed her bottom lip as she scanned the lyrics. 'It's beautiful.'

'I don't want to do it alone.'

'So we'll ask Hannah, we'll sing it together, the three of us.'

I didn't deserve for people to be so nice. As Hannah, Jordan and I studied the new music together, the concert rehearsal went on around us. In one corner of the stage I could hear Lucas practising the guitar solo that he'd taken over from Logan. In another, Parker wiped his hands on his dark T-shirt before uncoiling heavy cable and plugging wires into a battery of sockets lined up along the front of the stage. 'Did anyone see Ezra?' he yelled to some guys out of view backstage. 'I need some help here!'

Halfway through the rehearsal, right after Jordan and I sang the backing vocals for Christian, Miss Jones called a break. She gave us fifteen minutes – time for me to split from Jordan to get some air. 'Are you feeling OK?' she called after me.

I was heading across the stage, aiming for the side door. 'A little dizzy,' I admitted, pushing at the big exit sign.

Outside I needed my sunglasses again. I'd reached into the inside pocket of my jacket and put them on before I saw Ezra Powell leaning into a red saloon car to talk to the driver. A couple of seconds later it registered in my slow brain that the red car had a buckled roof and it belonged to JakB. A stab of alarm made me hurry across.

'Ezra, don't talk to him, he's crazy!' I warned. 'If he's asking for a ticket, don't give it to him!'

'Too late, baby. I got a backstage pass.' JakB reached out to show me the square of blue paper in his fist. He waved it in my face then snatched it away before I had time to grab it.

'Why did you do that?' I turned on Ezra, for the first time realizing that maybe he and JakB had some silent bond – hence the shared taste in black goth T-shirts. 'This guy is seriously weird. Hannah informed Miss Jones about him. We don't want him anywhere near the concert.'

'Says the law according to Darina.' Ezra swatted me off, then stood back to let JakB pocket his pass and roar away.

I could see Ezra's smirking lips but not the eyes behind the dark glasses.

'It's cool, Darina. I had a spare pass. Where's the problem?'

As I watched the back of Crazy Fan's car disappear out of the school grounds, I flipped. 'The problem is you, Ezra. You live in a techie bubble. If you took a look around and listened for one second to what people were saying you'd know that the guy is a total freak!'

'So let the security guys handle him,' Ezra shrugged. 'If he steps out of line, that is.'

'If!' I yelled. 'The guy is *permanently* out of line. Didn't you hear me? He hassled Hannah, he came to my house and tried to climb through my bedroom window. Go read his comments on the angelvoice website, come back, look me in the face and tell me he's sane.'

'You're overreacting.' Ezra didn't wipe the smirk off his face. In fact, it was plain he was enjoying this.

'OK, you want to know more about the freak you just invited through the door? He's death obsessed. He thinks he can communicate with Summer beyond the grave – he actually said it. And you know something, he could even be the guy who went to the mall and pulled the trigger on Summer!'

Ezra gave this time for thought, turned to walk away

then came back. 'Is there any evidence?' he asked. 'Or is this another Darina law you just made up?'

Through the rest of Monday and all of Tuesday I stayed lost in Summer's music.

In the school theatre, in between run-throughs of the tribute concert songs, Jordan, Hannah and I perfected 'Time to Go'. Back home, I continued to work on 'Red Sky' and 'Invisible'. This way I successfully blocked thoughts of the Beautiful Dead.

On Tuesday evening I opened my closet doors to decide what to wear for Logan's funeral, taking out a short black skirt and plain grey top. I would wear these with black tights and my knee-high black boots with the straps and silver studs – Logan always said he liked those boots. I was looking through the contents of my jewellery box for a silver necklace when the TV in the corner made a shock announcement.

'*Breaking news on the Scott Fichtner serial killings,*' the link person on Allyson Taylor's news station announced. The strip of moving text on the bottom of the screen confirmed the name. '*Police in Brooklyn have released without charge the suspect in two fatal shootings. They say that twenty-year-old Fichtner, who has a history of mental illness, is an attention-seeking fantasist and there is no hard evidence to connect him with either the Venice incident or the homicide in New Jersey. This blows wide open police investigations into the two shootings, plus several other copycat incidents . . .'*

I switched off the TV and sat down on my bed to absorb the news. How did that happen? How had I managed to convince myself one hundred and ten per cent that Fichtner was guilty?

Because I'd *wanted* it to be true, that's how. I'd told myself that Fichtner would cave in under police questioning and there would be a confession before the Saturday anniversary, because that way Summer and her parents got the peace they needed, the freedom to move on without me needing to act.

Idiot! I told myself. I hadn't let this happen with Jonas or Arizona – I'd stayed right in the middle of the action. This time though, the mall shooting had felt too random and overwhelming – and then there was Logan.

Logan comes first. I battled my way out of the new confusion by focusing on tomorrow's event. *If I get through the funeral then I'll drive out to Foxton and pick up the pieces, talk to Summer and start over.*

I'd gone back to sorting through my necklace box when Phoenix appeared. For the first time ever we didn't fall into each other's arms.

He stood by the door, waiting for me to speak. The

whole of his being – his aura – gave off a feeling of fear and doubt.

I watched him closely as the light faded. He was the same – tall, graceful, very beautiful with his pale, almost translucent skin – but totally different. 'You heard the news about Fichtner?' I asked coolly.

Phoenix nodded. He didn't move from his place at the far side of the room. 'Hunter sent me.'

'Of course he did. Now go ahead, tell me from him how I got it all wrong, wasted everyone's time, put Summer's eternal future in danger . . .'

'Darina, don't.'

'Don't what?'

'Don't do this.'

'Don't do what, Phoenix? What exactly am I doing that I'm not supposed to be doing?'

'You're locking me out. It's tearing me apart.'

Flipping the lid of my jewellery box shut, I went across to the window. '*I'm* locking *you* out! How come you held back the truth during the storm and lied to me about Logan? Were you scared to say what really happened because you knew how I'd react?'

'I didn't lie,' he said quietly, as if he didn't expect me to believe him.

'Whatever. Logan died in the hospital, did you know?

Yeah, sure you did.'

He gazed at me without answering, his eyes full of hurt.

'Can't you even say sorry?' I said, sobbing out the words. I never in a million years thought that it would be like this – that I would be fighting with Phoenix, that all the love and trust between us would be blown away like dust.

'Hunter sends a message,' he said, his voice emotionless. 'Now that Fichtner isn't a suspect, he wants you to go to my house.'

'Tell him I'm busy,' I replied, turning my back. 'I have a funeral to go to.'

'Hunter didn't say don't go to the funeral,' Phoenix reminded me. 'All he's saying is, visit my brother before it's too late.'

'And suddenly Brandon is going to take me into his confidence, tell me everything he knows about the dirty drugs deals that his buddy Oscar Thorne is mixed up in? He's going to 'fess up to being involved in vendettas and guns and all the insane, crazy stuff guys do when they're off their heads on illegal substances – yeah sure, Brandon is totally ready to do that.'

'Darina, listen to me—'

'You don't even care about Logan, do you?' There was

187

an elephant in the room and I couldn't ignore it. 'I was at the hospital with him, he was hooked up to tubes, in a coma—'

'I do care.'

'No, you admitted you were jealous of Logan and that's the truth. He didn't fit your picture of me being devoted to you for ever and ever. The way you saw it, there was always a chance that he would step into your shoes.'

'Yes, it's true,' Phoenix admitted softly, eyes downcast, still standing uncertainly in the spot where he'd materialized. 'I told you – it hurts to let you live your life, even though I know you have to move forward when this is over.'

The words crashed down on me like an avalanche: 'when this is over'. When we found all the answers for Jonas, Arizona, Summer and finally Phoenix, when the Beautiful Dead were free to leave. I was crushed by the weight of it, the knowledge that one day it would surely end.

'I'm guilty,' Phoenix told me, coming to me at last. 'I want to be bigger than I am, but I can't do it.'

I looked up into his hurting eyes. 'But I didn't love Logan that way, I loved him in a different way . . . I don't want to let him down by saying this stuff. I'm all mixed up.'

188

'It's too raw. Wait until after the funeral, then we can talk.'

I nodded. He was close to me, I was breathing him in but still resisting. The embers of my anger still glowed.

'About the visit to my house,' Phoenix mumbled. 'It's not Brandon that Hunter wants you to talk with, it's Zak.'

'Logan was like a lot of kids we know. He didn't follow any recognized faith, he just had a clear, natural sense of the difference between right and wrong.'

Byron Lavelle had chosen our music teacher, Katie Jones, to speak at the open-air funeral service. She was someone Logan liked, who we all looked up to. Now she stood on a hillside under a stand of tall redwoods, her hands folded in front of her, speaking to hundreds of people who had come to mourn Logan's passing.

'We all have our special memories,' Miss Jones continued. 'People have come forward with stories of Logan out at Hartmann Lake, casting a line far out into the clear water, of Logan chilling with the guys in a cabin out at Foxton. They say he never pushed himself to the front of the line, but would always listen and offer to help, even before he was asked.'

The casket lay two metres from where Hannah, Jordan and I stood. It was an eco-casket, this was an eco-burial, straight into non-consecrated ground – surprising choices by Logan's dad. Among the mourners were Logan's teachers, fellow students and friends like me who had known him since kindergarten.

'I have talked with scores of people,' Miss Jones said, 'and not a single one has had a bad word to say about Logan Lavelle.'

It came time for us to step forward to sing 'Time to Go'. Jordan, Hannah and I began with faint voices and fingers that fumbled the chords. But we owed it to Logan to do this, to make it the best song ever, so we looked towards the clear blue sky, gathered strength and sang from the bottom of our hearts to make him proud.

When we finished, I reached out to skim my fingers across the smooth white lid of the casket, then stepped to one side.

'Your song was beautiful.' Heather Madison came up to me at the close of the service. People were turning to wander slowly down the hillside, away from the peace of the place that would be for ever Logan's.

I smiled at her, glad that she'd made it here today. 'Summer wrote it.'

'I knew it was hers, the moment I heard the first notes.'

'It must have been the last one she wrote. I found her handwritten copy.'

Slipping Summer's paper from my pocket, I offered it to Heather. 'Please take it,' I said. 'It belongs with you.'

Jon Madison came alongside and gently took the paper from me. 'Thank you, Darina,' he told me. Then, putting his arm around his wife, he walked her down the hill.

I stayed until almost everyone had gone. I liked the way the pine trees stood tall and straight like soldiers guarding the place. I liked the stillness.

'Walk with me,' Logan's dad said at last.

Our feet crunched over the pink sandy ground, the granite rocks sparkled in the sun. Looking back, I saw the tops of the redwoods sway slightly in the breeze.

I hadn't expected the Rohrs to be there, and I only spotted them – Sharon, Brandon and Zak – when Byron Lavelle and I reached the National Forest car park at the bottom of the hill.

Sharon was the one who came forward to shake Byron's hand, telling him how sorry she was, then letting the unspoken bond between two parents who had each lost a son develop in silence.

Brandon hung back, obviously not eager to engage and probably only there because his mother had pressured him. Zak likewise. I made the usual comparison between Brandon and Phoenix – they had the same deep-set grey eyes, both were tall, but after that Brandon came off way worse. He was thicker set, more heavily muscled and less graceful, plus the biker leathers always gave him an aggressive edge. I went off on a tangent, picturing Phoenix in my mind's eye, almost hearing his voice in the rustle of the wind in the pines.

I swear I wouldn't have stepped forward to talk with Zak like Phoenix had told me except that Brandon unknowingly set it up for me. As Sharon accepted a ride home with Byron and walked away with him, Brandon turned to Zak and said, 'Kid, how about taking a ride in Darina's convertible?'

Zak shook his head. 'I'll ride the Harley with you.'

'Not an option. I have to be somewhere. Darina's heading your way, isn't that right, Darina?'

'Sure.'

'So go,' Brandon ordered, and he too walked quickly away.

'What's the problem – you think I'll bite?' I asked Zak.

He was trailing behind me, scuffing his shoes in the dirt.

'Get in,' I told him. I'd started to wonder why the hell Hunter wanted me to talk with the monosyllabic, moody kid. 'And by the way, did I ever hear a thank you for talking to Jardine and getting you off the fire-setting rap?'

Zak's eyelids flickered shut. 'I can take care of myself,' he grunted.

'Sure you can. That's why you hang out with Jacob and Taylor, the big bad guys, because nothing scares you, huh?' I started the engine and glanced sideways at my passenger. 'You want to know something?'

'No, but I guess I'm going to hear it anyway.'

I reversed out on to the track then pointed the car in the direction of town. 'I had a talk with Brandon the other day. He's freaked out that you're using him as a role model.'

As we joined the highway, Zak struck a pose, winding down the window and leaning his elbow on the car door. The wind pushed his hair back from his face making him look somehow softer-featured and younger.

'Why would that concern Brandon?' I persisted. 'What does Big Bro do that he doesn't want you to copy?'

'Brandon's a jerk,' Zak said suddenly and with genuine anger. 'He thinks he's a big player. Like, yeah!'

'You two had a fight?' I asked. I realized I could mine this seam and with luck I'd strike gold.

Zak shrugged. 'He pushes me around – do this, don't do that.'

'And he's not even your dad. I get it.'

'He's nothing. A big fat zero.'

'That's not what I hear. I hear he's well connected.'

'We're talking Brandon here, right?'

'He got me this car,' I pointed out. 'It's a high-end machine.'

'Yeah, from his dope-dealing buddy,' Zak muttered. 'I just found out – Will Stone owed Brandon big time, that's why he gave him the car.'

Whoa – I was driving a vehicle belonging to a drugs dealer! Suddenly it didn't seem so shiny red and desirable, but I registered the name, Will Stone, and stored it.

Now that he'd started, Zak was on a roll. It seemed to me there was a mountain of resentment for the kid to off-load. 'Then what,' he went on, 'the next time Stone asks Brandon a favour . . . ?'

'When did he last ask him?' I cut in.

'Last year. It was some crap about delivering a package to a guy called Oscar. Brandon tells Stone no, and that's how come—'

'Will Stone had to deliver the package himself?'

Zak nodded. 'Which is why Oscar Thorne was sitting in Starbucks waiting for Stone the day—'

'That Summer Madison was shot.' I ended his sentence for him, turned off the highway and delivered Zak right to his door.

This was big. Zak's information put two pieces of lowlife in the right place at the right time, and it was down to me to carry the facts back to Foxton.

Any other time except the day of Logan's funeral I would have hit the highway and been out there before sunset.

Tonight was way different. Instead of parking my car and walking down from the ridge and across the yard to hear the barn door banging in the wind, I sat in my room listening to Summer's demo disc. *Tomorrow, after rehearsal*, I told myself. *It'll be soon enough.*

And no one appeared in a halo of silver light to tell me otherwise.

'About yesterday,' Miss Jones announced next day before the last-but-one rehearsal began. 'I was so proud.'

There was silence in the theatre. Parker halted his sound check. Even Ezra dumped the coils of cable he was carrying and slouched across to listen.

'It was the hardest thing,' Miss Jones said. 'Especially for you three girls – Hannah, Darina and Jordan. You came through for Logan.'

It was Lucas who led the applause. He started slowly and soon others joined in, turning towards us with serious expressions, letting us know how they agreed with our music teacher until she stepped in and reminded everyone it was time to rehearse.

'Jeez,' Hannah mumbled, wiping her eyes with the back of her hand.

I dabbed more carefully around the edges of my mascara. 'Give me your laptop,' I sniffed. 'Let me take a look at angelvoice, see who posted comments.'

So I hid away in a corner, expecting to find excited Summer fans looking ahead to the concert. Sure enough – *Can't wait till Saturday*, Zoe Zee wrote. Skygirl followed up with: *It's gonna be awesome.*

JakB came in with his usual sick stuff. *You heard the news? Another kid from Ellerton High got buried. Who cares? The big thing is – Summer lives!*

I jumped up from my seat when I read that and ran over to Ezra to make him read it too. 'This is the guy you gave the backstage pass to!' I told him. 'This is one sick psycho.'

'Back off, Darina,' was Ezra's response, tipping his shades higher up the bridge of his nose – a kind of repetitive geeky gesture he had. 'The guy can express an opinion, can't he?'

'No, he can't!' I followed him backstage. 'You're going to go out of here and find him, take away his pass, end of story.'

Ezra shook his head. 'What's the big deal?'

'The deal is, JakB seriously needs help. Someone has to tell him he can't act this way.'

Ezra escaped from the corner I'd backed him into. 'This is a free country,' he said, not looking where he was going and barging into Parker.

'Read this!' I said, thrusting the laptop under Parker's nose. 'The stuff about Logan dying and nobody caring. Tell Ezra it's sick.'

'No comment,' Parker muttered, making space for Ezra to squeeze past. But then he got how mad I was and tried to calm me down. 'Don't expect sympathy from Ezra,' he told me. 'He and Logan weren't best buddies, remember.'

'Oh yeah, the fight outside the theatre. What was that about exactly?'

'I have no clue. I only know it didn't end there. It blew up again in the cabin that night . . .'

'Ezra and Logan had another fight?'

'No fists were used,' Parker corrected me in a mocking, school-teacher voice. 'They yelled at one another then Ezra made his exit.'

'Out into the storm?' I asked.

'We're talking seventy-mile-per-hour winds,' he agreed. 'But Ezra totally lost it. He swore Logan was a jerk, then he was out of there.'

'Nice,' I muttered. 'So who's going to deal with crazy man JakB on Saturday night, now that your bonehead buddy gave him a backstage pass?'

My heart wasn't in the rehearsal. I went through the motions, my mind flying ahead to the point where I'd be heading out to Foxton at last, wondering how Summer would be and how I would feel about Phoenix now that the line had been drawn under Logan's funeral. Meanwhile, I sang my songs, then left the theatre without stopping to talk with Hannah and Jordan.

Sick in my stomach, I drove my druggie boy's toy out of town, running through the new facts I'd learned from Zak. I was hoping to see Summer without running into Hunter and the others, also dreading another clash with Phoenix. I paid no attention to the sun on the granite rocks to either side of the highway, or to the big blue sky above.

I reached the ridge and Hunter was waiting for me, statue-still among the fluttering aspens. He greeted me with an impassive expression, then surprised me when he said. 'Hello, Darina. I'm sorry about Logan.'

I nodded and took a sharp intake of breath.

'I mean it. He was a good friend.'

'The best.' I walked on under the trees, calming myself with the soft, whispering breeze running through the canopy of fresh green leaves.

'And I have to thank you for not pursuing my family history.'

'You made the situation pretty plain,' I muttered, then changed the subject. 'Where's Summer?'

'In the barn, waiting for you.'

We walked down the hill together, him keeping pace with my shorter stride, saying nothing, but giving me the intense stare which meant he was busy reading my mind. When we reached the weed-strewn yard, he stepped out across my path. 'Summer has only forty-eight hours here on the far side,' he said quietly. 'Two days for you to find her killer.'

'And if I don't?' My voice quivered over the biggest mystery of all.

'We fail,' Hunter said, staring steadily into my eyes.

'She's back in limbo.'

'Unable to rest,' I sighed. *A soul in permanent torment.*

Hunter read the thought. 'Exactly that.' He paused to let this settle inside my throbbing head. 'The consequences are huge. And don't think we can do what we did as a last resort with Jonas and Arizona.'

'You mean, time-travel back to the day of Summer's death to let her relive the event?'

He nodded.

'Why not? If this new Will Stone lead doesn't work out, and JakB slips through the net too, we may need to take her back.'

'Not possible,' Hunter insisted. 'It's too painful. She's not strong enough.'

I frowned. 'Even if there's no other option?'

He took me by the arm and walked me down the side of the barn into an old corral with broken fencing and tall yellow Indian tobacco plants growing through the cracks in the flattened, parched earth. 'You're not listening,' he said impatiently. 'Time travel is the hardest thing we Beautiful Dead get to do, and even the other stuff – the storm of beating wings, the memory zap, the appearing and disappearing – they take a lot of supernatural strength, which Summer no longer has.'

'But if she rests up . . .'

'Not possible.'

'If you help her . . .'

'Still not possible. Each restless soul who is permitted to return to the far side has an individual store of energy. If I tell you that Summer may not even make it through to Saturday, then do you understand what I'm saying?'

'I do now,' I whispered, pulling away from the overlord and retracing my steps to the front of the barn. 'I need to see her, work through some new ideas.'

'Go ahead,' Hunter said, standing on the spot, watching me drag open the huge, creaking door.

The moment I saw Summer, I knew all too clearly what Hunter meant.

She sat on the steps to the hay loft, the long, dark-green silk skirt that she'd worn on the day of the shooting billowing out over her ankles and feet. Her blonde hair cascaded around a face so thin and shadowed that it seemed impossible that she was still here with me on the far side. I walked quickly across the straw-strewn floor to sit beside her.

Slowly Summer turned her head and fixed her heavily lashed eyes on me, the rich violet irises now darkened to midnight blue, the pupils enormous. 'You sang my song at Logan's service,' she murmured in a voice almost too faint to hear.

I nodded. 'Your mom loved it. I guess she felt you and she were close again.'

'Thank you, Darina.'

'I'm sorry I haven't been here for you these last few days.' The words didn't go anywhere near to expressing the wrung-out, strung-out guilt and despair that had entered my heart since I set eyes on her.

'No need to be sorry. You've worked so hard, and it was always a long-shot that we'd find my killer.'

'But listen – I picked up some new information. There's a guy called Will Stone, a dealer. And a guy named Oscar Thorne. There was a fight for territory, or some big drugs deal that went wrong. Stone wanted to deliver a packet. They were both in the mall the day you were shot.'

'And I got in the way?' Summer whispered.

'My plan is to go back and talk to the cop, Henry Jardine, like he asked me to. I'll push Thorne and Stone's names into the centre of the frame. Thorne is already in jail – I'm thinking that Jardine can put the pressure on him, maybe offer him an early-release deal in return for information that would nail Stone. So no more violence, in case you were still worried about that.'

'Sounds good.' Summer smiled briefly before a frown creased her pale forehead.

'And tomorrow I'll track down JakB,' I promised. 'He's the guy who's coming up with all the crazy comments on your website. Plus I've seen him in the creepy flesh – he could definitely be our guy.'

'Also good,' she sighed, leaning her head against the rough plank wall. 'But you know, what matters is that you tried. I won't turn against you if you don't come up with the answer.'

She closed her eyes and I felt her drift, almost as if the last micro-gram of energy had drained away. When I took her hand in mine it was ice cold. 'Don't give up,' I pleaded. 'Two days – we still have forty-eight hours to solve this!'

Misery weighed me down as I walked back up to the water tower. I'd made promises, begged with Summer to hang on, while my heart was secretly gripped with giant doubts.

I stopped to lean against the blackened, rusting uprights of the tower, seeming to hear the words of Summer's last song echoing around the hillsides. *There's a hill / I'll wait until / The stars appear / And the sky grows clear.* In the distance, the dark, conical shape of Angel Rock seemed like a long-robed figure in prayer. *Then it's time for me to go.*

Dusk was gathering over Amos Peak when Phoenix joined me, the sky a deep shade of purple, the mountains darkening into jagged outline.

My already bruised, battered heart was squeezed again.

He stood by my side, waiting.

'Did Hunter tell you to come?' I asked, almost taunting him.

'No.'

'So you came because you wanted to?'

'I asked him.'

'Yeah, don't forget to ask Hunter for permission,' I mocked.

He ducked his head backwards as if I'd thrown a punch, but he stayed silent.

'Sorry. You didn't deserve that.' I walked out from under the shadow of the tower, amongst sweet grasses and pale-blue flowers along the ridge.

Phoenix watched me go, letting the distance between us grow, waiting for me to turn around.

I had only one question battling its way to the surface, and Phoenix didn't need any telepathic super-power to know what it was. I kept my back towards him as I spoke it out loud. 'Who was it – you or Dean?'

'Me or Dean what?'

'You know. Was it you who set up the barrier that pushed Logan from the rock, or was it Dean?'

'Neither.'

I turned and strode back along the ridge. 'So it was the storm?' I demanded. 'A force of nature killed him?'

'Believe me. We were across the valley, checking the Government Bridge camp ground.'

I held my breath, stared into his beautiful grey eyes. 'You're saying the wind battered him, pushed him over the edge?'

'Maybe. I don't know for sure. I wasn't there.'

'But you know everything!' I cried. 'One of you – Iceman or Donna, you or Dean – must have seen it happen, or at least heard it.'

'None of us.'

'And you couldn't save him?' I remembered the rain and the howling wind, Logan's white car parked in my usual place, the panic in my heart as I found him lying almost dead at the foot of the rock. 'Why are you standing here now, looking at me like that?'

'I'm waiting for the pain to ease.'

'For me to come back to you?' It was as if I was on a wild, lonely journey, in the middle of a vast emptiness.

'You only have to believe me,' Phoenix said.

'How can I?'

'Ask yourself, did I ever lie to you? In all the time you knew me before I died, I never hid anything from you. The same since.'

I was close, studying his smooth skin, his clear eyes, the downward sweep of his dark hair. I was back in a place where I could let his heart speak.

Then he was holding me – softly at first, then tightly, locking his hands together in the small of my back, pulling me towards him.

I was off balance, swept back in by the force of my love for him, letting it open my closed mind. The thrill when he kissed me ran through my lips, down my spine, reaching every part of me.

'In the end you'll leave me,' I murmured, holding hands with Phoenix and walking between the slim, silver trunks of the aspens. A crescent moon rose in the indigo sky, the pole star shone bright.

'Try not to think that way. Remember we still have some time together.'

'Will I come back to Foxton in a year's time?' I wondered. 'What happens when I finally walk down to the barn and there's no one there except ghosts?'

'Say my name out loud,' he told me. 'You won't see me but I'll be here.'

'You promise? I've prayed – often – for you to haunt me. I couldn't bear for you to go away and never come back.'

He stopped and raised his hand to stroke my cheek. 'It won't happen. Come looking for me, Darina, and you'll find me here. Always.'

11

Brandon Rohr was the type who didn't get up before midday, but he was there at my door early next morning.

I was leaving the house for our final concert rehearsal, under so much pressure since my last trip out to Foxton that I'd skipped the normal things like sleeping and eating and was still in the clothes I'd worn for the previous twenty-four hours. When I saw Brandon leaning against my car in the drive, my first thought was that he was through doing me favours and was there to collect the keys. I held them up for him to grab.

'Get in,' he said, opening the driver's door for me. Then he went and sat in the passenger seat. 'Drive,' he grunted.

'I have a rehearsal,' I began weakly.

'This is short,' he promised. He waited for me to reach the end of the street then delivered his message in plain, one syllable words. 'Don't go near Will Stone.'

I took my foot off the pedal and stalled the car. 'Who? I don't know what you mean.'

'Zak's a loser,' Brandon said calmly. 'But he's family. How long do you think it took him to admit what he'd leaked to you?'

'Thirty minutes?' I guessed. 'Don't tell me – blood is thicker than water, he was stricken with guilt and spilled everything.'

'Right on target.' Waiting for me to re-start the car, he studied me closely. 'You're just a kid, Darina.'

'Yeah, thanks for patronizing me,' I muttered back, turning the corner and cruising through town towards school.

'You and Phoenix – I wonder how it would've worked out.'

I took my eyes off the road to stare back. 'He loved me. I loved him.'

He shrugged. 'Maybe it would've been enough, who knows?'

I know! I thought. I still practically had the feel of Phoenix's arms around me, the taste of his lips on mine from the night before.

'Whatever. I'm still saying, stay away from Will Stone.'

'Even if it turns out that he's the guy who

shot Summer Madison?'

'Stop the car!' Suddenly Brandon grabbed the wheel, steered me up the kerb on to the sidewalk and slammed on the handbrake. 'I'm not asking where you got that idea; I already know. I'm telling you word for word what I told Zak – Stone is a heavyweight, the real deal. If he hears a whisper that you're poking your nose into his business, you're history – get it?'

I stared at Brandon until my eyes felt like they were popping out of my head. What had happened to his cool-guy persona, and where had this freaked-out guy come from? I mean, Brandon's hand was still on the brake and it was shaking.

'Darina, don't mess with Stone.'

'I'm not scared,' I tried to say.

He grabbed my wrist. '*Be* scared!' he warned. 'If Will Stone hears that you're saying his name in the same breath as Summer Madison, he won't think twice.'

'OK, I hear you.' Brandon was hurting my wrist. 'I won't do anything stupid.' I meant what I said. In any case, wasn't I planning on handing everything over to Jardine?

'No, listen. You won't just not do anything stupid. You won't do *anything*!'

'OK, cool.' I was trying to twist my arm out of his grasp

211

and failing. All the time I was thinking, *Brandon is up to his neck in this shit and that's why he's trying to scare me.* I wasn't thinking that what he was saying was fact.

Maybe he knew he wasn't getting through because he suddenly let go of me and flung open the car door. He got out, slammed it shut and walked off without looking back. I got back on the road and arrived at rehearsal with five minutes to spare.

As last run-throughs go, this one was easy. Miss Jones wanted to make a change and bring in 'Time to Go' as the new final number – she checked that we all felt OK about this, then rehearsed it with me, Jordan and Hannah singing the verses and everyone joining in on the chorus. There was a hitch on some lighting cues, but apart from that everything ran smoothly and we were out of the theatre by eleven-thirty. In my head, as I headed for the car park, I was already thinking ahead, picturing myself sitting in Jardine's office.

I never made it. JakB jumped out from behind the janitor's office and cut me off. He hooked one arm around my throat, slammed the other hand across my mouth and dragged me into an outbuilding containing grass-cutting machinery.

'Let go of me!' I yelled as I tried to bite his sweaty palm.

The storeroom was dark and windowless, I was trapped.

JakB flung me against the mower. 'You know what your crappy teacher did?' His voice came out strangled and hissy. 'She banned me from the concert. She banned me!'

'Don't blame me,' I croaked before I bit again – this time I got his forearm.

He slammed his fist into my stomach and I doubled up. 'She took away my pass, told Security don't let me anywhere near.'

'How do you know that?'

'I know! Now what do I do?'

I ducked the next punch aimed at my head. 'Stay away from me!'

'What do I do now?' Suddenly he lowered his fists and began to cry like a baby in the dark. 'What am I going to tell Summer? She won't believe they took away my pass.'

I tuned in, played it his way. 'Summer will understand,' I said between sharp, painful breaths. *Breathe. Look him in the eye.* 'She knows you care.'

JakB stopped snivelling as fast as he began. 'You think?' he sneered. 'Isn't it like it is in her song – I worship her but she doesn't even notice I'm there?'

Slowly I stood upright and edged away from the machinery towards the door. 'Sure she does. Summer cares about you, she cares about all her fans.'

'No one loves Summer the way I do,' he sighed, his outsized Adam's apple working up and down his skinny throat. 'I tell her that every single day.'

'And she hears you. She'll understand about the concert, believe me.'

'I have to go tell her again,' he decided, turning impulsively towards the door.

'Do it now,' I urged, blocking a strong image of him crouched by Summer's grave spilling his insane guts, saying whatever crazy stuff whirled inside his demented brain.

'No – later,' he argued, turning back towards me. 'These days I keep her waiting, the way she used to make me wait. "You acted like I was invisible," I tell her. "All those emails – you never replied."'

Take a deep breath. Don't try to predict his next move. JakB went up-down, up-down and he was making my flesh creep big time.

'She laughs at me, tells me she has a thousand emails. But the others didn't mean anything. It's me who loves her best.'

'She knows that,' I whispered. I was near the door but not near enough. My heart was hammering, I could hardly breathe.

So I'd never in my life been so glad to see anyone as

when Ezra pulled open that door and stepped inside.

'Dude, you need to let Darina walk out of here,' Ezra said calmly. Daylight flooded into the storeroom. I was out of danger.

'They took away my pass,' JakB whined, wiping his cheeks with the back of his hand.

'I know. I'm the guy who told you,' Ezra reminded him. 'It doesn't follow that you harm Darina. How does that help?'

'She hates me. She went to the teacher and took away my pass.'

'Yeah, that's what Darina does – steps into areas that don't concern her. It's a bad habit.'

As my breath came back and the pain in my stomach eased, I started to protest. 'Ezra, for God's sake let me out of here! I warned you about this guy and you wouldn't listen.'

'Hey, how about thanking me for rescuing you?' He did that tipping his shades up his nose thing and gave that smirk.

'Yeah – thanks. Now let me out.'

We all three emerged from the storeroom into the car park, me still breathing hard and JakB looking drained and exhausted. Only Ezra kept his cool. 'Dude, get out of here,' he told the maniac, who walked unsteadily towards his car. Then Ezra fixed his attention on me. 'Bad mistake,' he muttered.

'Me?' I demanded.

'To mess with a guy like that.'

'I told you he was crazy. You're the one who fixed for him to come to the concert.'

'*Because* he's crazy,' Ezra explained. 'Think about it. Give him what he wants and he's not a problem. Take it away from him and he gets out a gun and shoots people.'

I gasped long and hard then nodded. 'Exactly!' I yelled, relieved in a way that Ezra got my point, but scared too. 'JakB didn't get Summer, and he wanted her more than anything.'

Ezra shrugged, ignoring my major point and getting ready to move off when he saw Lucas heading our way. 'Like I said – bad mistake to take away his pass.'

'Darina, are you OK?' Since Logan, Lucas seemed to be stepping into the role of best platonic buddy and I was truly grateful. 'Was there a problem with Ezra?'

'No, it's cool.'

'What about the other guy?'

'Yeah, there was an incident.' Briefly I gave Lucas the details and allowed him to walk me to my car. 'How come you thought Ezra was the problem?' I asked.

Lucas got into the car beside me. 'No reason,' he mumbled, coughing and clearing his throat.

Not good enough. I always knew when Lucas was hiding something – for a start his face turned bright red. 'Actually, to tell you the truth, Ezra *was* mixed up in that last little incident. He's the one who implicated me in Miss Jones's decision to take away JakB's pass.'

'Nice!' Lucas's response was sharper than I expected. 'You want me to talk with him, tell him to keep his nose clean in future?'

I shook my head. 'No thanks. And listen, Lucas, right now I have to be somewhere . . .'

'You don't get rid of me so easy,' he insisted. 'I plan to ride with you to your house, make sure you arrive safe.'

'You think JakB is still hanging around?' Glancing round the car park, I saw that his red car had gone and that Ezra's Toyota was also leaving by the main exit. 'See – all clear!'

'Drive, Darina,' Lucas insisted. 'There are a couple of things I need to tell you.'

I didn't head straight home with Lucas. Instead, I drove through Centennial towards Hartmann Lake, stopping on the overlook when Lucas's story got really interesting.

'You want to know why Logan and Ezra had that

second fight?' he asked. 'It was over you again, Darina.'

'No way!' I was staring across the wide valley, down at the lake.

'I'm serious. Out at the cabin on the night of the storm, and earlier, outside the theatre . . .'

'They fought over me?' I repeated.

'Ezra made a bad comment and Logan reacted.'

'What kind of comment?'

Lucas screwed up his mouth in embarrassment. 'The kind guys make about a girl's reputation.'

'He called me cheap? How did you find out? I thought no one knew why Logan fought with Ezra.'

'That's the way Logan wanted it. He didn't want the comment repeated.'

'So it was bad,' I sighed. 'I kind of picked up that Ezra didn't like me, but—'

'No,' Lucas interrupted. 'That's the point, Darina. Ezra *did* like you – a lot!'

'Oh my God!' I was having to paint a whole new picture and at this stage the brush strokes were broad, the details blurred. 'Ezra liked me!'

'A year ago, before you dated Phoenix, he had a crush.'

'Ezra?' The geek in the goth T-shirt, the tongue-tied guy at the school prom who never got himself a date. For Ezra Powell, think in stereotypes.

'Then Phoenix came along and blew him out of the water.'

'Ezra was never *in* the water!'

Lucas was quiet for a while. 'Did you ever think how hard it is for a guy like Ezra?' he asked.

I breathed out sharply. 'Yeah – sorry.'

'So, he's hurt that you were never into him. OK – correction, he's hurt that you never even *noticed* him.'

'To argue my corner, Lucas, I never thought I was the type of girl a guy would have a crush on. I'm not an Arizona or a Jordan.'

There was another long silence from the passenger seat. 'I'm never going to understand women,' he said at last, making me smile in spite of everything.

'So, Ezra is licking his wounds,' he went on. 'He's pretty fixated on you, according to what Logan told me. Then Phoenix—'

'Dies,' I cut in. 'And Ezra is ready again to make his move.'

'But this time Logan gets there first. He's your shoulder to cry on, your rock.'

'I knew Logan for ever,' I sighed. My throat constricted and tears welled up.

Lucas pushed on with the point he was making. 'So at this point, Ezra can't take any more. One day he's ready to die for you, the next he's turned one hundred and eighty degrees.'

'He hates me?'

'That's the kind of guy he is. He makes a habit of running after girls he knows he can't have – you, Arizona, Summer . . .'

'He had crushes on all of us?'

Lucas nodded. 'All inside his head, never any real action.'

'And he ends up bitter and twisted, bitching about us?'

'And choosing the wrong guy to offload on.'

'Logan.' And now I got the picture – all the details. Ezra calls me cheap to Logan's face and like a medieval knight Logan fights to defend me, not once but twice. 'Lucas, out at the cabin – did you hear what Ezra said?'

'Some of it.' He was turning red again and staring down at the glittering water of the distant lake. 'Logan and Ezra were in the kitchen. Ezra claimed he'd . . .'

'What?'

'He'd . . .'

'*Had* me?'

Now that I'd said it, Lucas felt able breathe again. 'He started in on the detail. Logan grabbed him and threw him out.'

220

'I never . . . he didn't!' I whispered.

'I know that, Darina. Logan knew that. But you need to watch out for Ezra, is all I'm saying. He's out to cause problems and there's no Logan to protect you any more.

JakB was an extreme version of Ezra Powell, and now I saw why Ezra took on board the crazy fan's reasoning. *They wear matching T-shirts,* I reminded myself darkly.

After Hartmann, I'd dropped Lucas off at his house and insisted on driving home alone. I'd thanked him for telling me the truth and said I'd see him the next morning before the concert. Meanwhile, I was still on my way to Deputy Sheriff Jardine's office.

'The deputy sheriff is busy,' the officer at Reception told me when I went in.

'This is important,' I told her. I felt myself come up against that authority barrier that people in uniform present – the look across the desk that says: *You are a small, insignificant person unworthy of my full attention.* 'He would want to see me.'

'I would?' Jardine asked, coming through from his inner office and recognizing me right away. 'Thanks, Sheryl. I've got five minutes to give to Darina before I go off duty.'

'Go through,' Sheryl-in-uniform sniffed.

So I sat in Jardine's room eagerly spilling out all the Brandon-linked information he'd asked me for. I named Oscar Thorne and Will Stone, told him about the bad blood between the drugs gangs, the suppliers, the dealers, the middle men.

'So Stone was on his way to meet with Thorne in the mall?' Jardine checked with me. 'And now you want me to talk this through with Thorne?'

'Right now!' I said. 'You can't let this go through the weekend. It has to be today!'

I got the authority barrier again – the level, narrow-eyed look, the *tap-tap* of the pen against the desk. Then Jardine thrust out his bottom lip. 'Darina, did you ever think of a future career in the police department?' he asked.

'This isn't a joke. There's definitely a drugs link – you see what I'm saying?'

'That Thorne planned a shoot-out and your friend Summer was in the wrong place at the wrong time. Sure, I see. And I have to tell you, Darina, that on this occasion my senior officer was way ahead of you.'

This made me sit right back in my seat. 'And?'

Jardine checked the date on his multi-function wristwatch. 'Today's the twenty-ninth. That makes it the twenty-seventh when we pulled in Will Stone for interview.'

'And?' I said again, this time hardly audible.

'Stone had an alibi for the day Summer died. He was at the hospital, visiting his sick mother.'

'You believed him?' What a corny story – how could the cops be so gullible?

'It checked out. Even the heads of drugs cartels have sick mothers, you know. Plus, we got a warrant to search Stone's property, including the contents of his gun closet. There was no weapon there that matched the gun responsible for Summer's death.'

'So he got rid of it. That doesn't prove anything.'

Jardine clicked his tongue against the roof of his mouth. 'But the alibi, Darina . . .'

'He was at the hospital at the exact time Summer died?'

'Check. Stone texted Thorne to say he couldn't make Starbucks, that his mother was in the ER and they had to make a new time to meet. It's all on record.'

I closed my eyes, tried to breathe evenly, felt hope slip away. I clutched at one last straw. 'Maybe Stone got someone to deputize,' I suggested. 'Say he sent another member of the gang to do the deal with Thorne.'

Jardine sighed as he looked at his watch a second time. 'Go home, Darina,' he said. 'I'm into official me-time, ready to do some fishing.'

*   *   *

I seemed always to be in the car, always losing hope.

'What do I do now?' I asked out loud.

The hood was down, a wind was blowing and I was longing with all my heart for support from the Beautiful Dead.

'I'm out of ideas,' I confessed. 'There's only JakB left on my list, and the guy scares the crap out of me.'

Suddenly the weight of not sleeping and eating for two days, of picturing Summer in permanent torment, for ever in limbo, got through to me. 'Hunter, Phoenix, I need your help,' I begged.

When they didn't reply with invisible wings and halos of shimmering light I knew I'd been abandoned. I drifted through the streets, hardly knowing where I was, feeling the loneliest I'd ever felt in my life.

The isolation was intense – I was looking around for help and knowing that I was in this alone, that Summer had only me to rely on and time was racing on, sprinting towards the finish, running out.

The certainty sent me spiralling into a panic that made every normal thing on the road suddenly seem unreal and threatening. A woman stepped off the sidewalk without seeing me and making me swerve wide. She stood in the road acting like I was to blame. Then a guy on a Harley overtook on a bend, cutting back in front of me much too close. My foot hit the brake and my engine stalled for the second time that day.

By now my nerves were shredded. I re-started the car with a trembling hand, telling myself that the place to head was home and bed, but doing exactly the opposite by pointing the car in the direction of Deer Creek.

I drove on slowly, like I was in a dream, ignoring the horn blast of a Porsche driver who wanted me to pick up speed. As he overtook, I caught sight of a guy with a shaven head giving me the finger.

An angry guy with a gold wristwatch in a black Porsche. Will Stone maybe?

My unreliable mind cranked up my stress level another notch into undiluted paranoia. The local drugs baron was onto me – he already knew I'd spoken to the cops, he'd made it his business to learn every detail of my life – where I lived, who my friends were, what car I drove.

But no – the Porsche was past me and accelerating, the roar of his engine fading as he disappeared round the bend. Tears of relief trickled down my cheeks.

Don't cry while you drive – it should be in the Highway Code, along with using a cell phone and talking to the undead. I wept and by the time I reached Deer Creek I could hardly see the track. I parked in the spot where

Phoenix and I would always meet, where I'd waited for him the night he died.

'Hey, Darina,' he said, reaching out to open my car door.

It was midday and the sun was shining on Deer Creek. The water was crystal clear.

'Hold my hand,' I told Phoenix, and when he took it I shivered at the coldness of his touch. 'How did you know I'd be here?' I asked.

'It was more than a guess,' he admitted. 'I made it happen.'

'You planted the idea in my head?'

He nodded. 'It seemed a good place for us to meet.'

'It is.' I remembered deciding to drive home but inexplicably coming here instead. 'How long have you been around?'

'I took over from Dean after you left Jardine's office. There's been someone watching over you twenty-four/seven.'

'And I felt so alone,' I sighed. 'I wish sometimes you guys would give me a signal.'

'Against Hunter's orders,' he reminded me, leading me down to the water's edge then striding from rock to rock to reach a large boulder in the middle of the creek. He climbed on to it and offered me his hand to help me up. 'He figures someone from the far side might get suspicious.'

'Can't he take pity on me once in a while?' I stood unsteadily beside Phoenix on our favourite rock, dizzied by the smooth, strong flow of the water around the boulder. 'Truly, this is the worst I've been.'

'Hunter doesn't do pity,' he reminded me. 'His focus is on Summer.'

'How's she doing?'

'Not good. It's weird – she's shutting down.'

'Still giving up?' I asked. I held tight to his hand, scared by the current at our feet and remembering how weak Summer had been the last time I saw her.

Phoenix sat down on the rock, letting his legs dangle over the edge and inviting me to sit next to him. 'She's not fighting, she's kind of slipping away. I think she's ready to leave.'

'She can't do that – not until tomorrow. Tell her she has to give me another twenty-four hours.'

Phoenix tilted his head to one side, half looking away. 'It's hard to reach her. She sits on the steps in the barn but she's not there, she's a million miles away, drifting, losing contact.'

'Oh don't!' I cried. 'How did we get here, Phoenix? I had so many ideas on clearing up Summer's death but none of them worked out – Fichtner, Oscar Thorne and Will Stone—'

'There's still JakB,' he cut in.

I shook my head. 'I don't know any more. Sure, he's weird, but is he a killer? You know when he trapped me in the storeroom – he cried like a baby. I looked at him and I thought, No way is this guy capable of shooting the girl he worships.'

'But we don't know how his mind works. He's not like you and me, Darina. He lives in a fantasy world.'

'And we don't?' I asked, still clinging to Phoenix's hand and suddenly seeing the irony of the situation. 'You call this real?' *Me sitting in the middle of Deer Creek with my Beautiful Dead boyfriend.*

He smiled self-consciously. 'You know what I'm saying. If we're looking for an irrational psychopath, JakB exactly fills the slot.' Pausing for a while to look me straight in the eye, he reached out to stroke my hair. 'Don't do what Summer is doing, you don't surrender, you hear?'

'Is that what you see when you read my thoughts – surrender?'

He nodded. 'And failure. You figure you've let Summer down and it eats away at your confidence.'

'We have less than twenty-four hours,' I sighed. 'It's true, I do feel hopeless – deep, deep in the pit of my stomach.'

'That's not the way I see it,' he argued, leaning out over the water and watching our reflection. 'Look at what you achieved – a million times more than Summer ever expected.'

'Such as?'

'Such as making contact with her parents, working on the anniversary concert, dealing with Logan's funeral, plus following all the leads as soon as they were thrown up.'

'Not enough,' I muttered, feeling more and more drawn to the pull of the current beneath our feet. I imagined slipping into the water, feeling its icy touch as I sank down to the stony bed. 'Phoenix, I'm exhausted.'

So he wrapped me in his arms and softly kissed the top of my head. 'We used to swim here,' he reminded me. 'The water's deep, remember?'

'It made our skin tingle, even in summer.'

'There's a ledge on the far bank. We sunbathed.'

I nodded and let the memories wash over me of Phoenix when he was alive – his skin tanned, his flesh warm to the touch and a strong heart beating in his chest.

'I wanted to lie in the sun with you for ever. That's what love means to me, Darina – you, the sun, clear water.'

'I never asked you this before,' I said softly. 'Maybe I didn't want to know.'

229

'Asked me what?'

'Before me, before *us* – did you ever . . . were you ever in love?'

He paused for a while, then shrugged. 'I thought I was a couple of times at my last school – the usual crushes.'

'Yeah, I really don't want to hear it,' I said, backtracking like crazy. 'You're going to tell me they were blonde and beautiful size zeros.'

Phoenix's laugh was rare but when it came, like it did now, it was low down in his throat and covered me in a warm glow. 'The first girl was named Skye and she was dark-haired. Her dad designed websites for major car manufacturers. When I asked her out on a date she quizzed me over my dad's occupation. No dad, I said. So with Skye I was never out of the starting-blocks.'

'That's sad,' I said with a grin on my face. 'Number two?'

'Caroline Garrety. I spent six months worshipping her, having imaginary conversations, figuring out which movie we would see when I finally asked her out on a date.'

'And?'

'I asked her one Halloween to share a horror movie DVD at my place. She looked straight through me and told me no offence but she wasn't ready to start dating yet, thanks.'

'How old was she?'

'Eleven. I was twelve.'

'You're crazy!' I laughed.

'I love you,' he told me and kissed me until my breath was gone.

And in the background, just rising above the sound of water running over pebbles, I could hear Summer's voice singing her 'Red Sky' song about not having time to say goodbye.

12

There was no sleeping that night either – Summer's last one on the far side. But sleeping was what Hunter ordered for me, and he took Phoenix away so that I could rest.

'I won't sleep!' I protested when Phoenix got ready to leave. We were sitting in my car at the end of my street.

'You need to rest. And Hunter needs me back at Foxton Ridge. Donna is stuck in the barn taking care of Summer, so he wants me on patrol at the Government Bridge camp ground. He's expecting weekend visitors, and if they stumble across the old ranch house, they have a habit of getting curious.'

'I know,' I sighed. 'And the last thing you all need on Summer's final night is working to set up barriers against far-siders. I understand.'

Phoenix made it plain he didn't want to leave. 'We've already cruised the streets looking for JakB,' he reminded

232

me. 'You asked if anyone had seen him in the music stores, the cafés, all the places he might hang out. No one even knows he exists.'

'But he can't vanish off the face of the earth. He's around here somewhere.'

'Wait until tomorrow. If he's so crazy about getting into the concert, that's when he'll show up again.'

'You're right.' The low sun had left the streets in deep shadow, the light was grey and cool. 'I'll go home and check my laptop. Maybe something will show up.'

'Cool.' Thinking that he'd convinced me to stay indoors, Phoenix was ready to leave. He frowned and used his mysterious energy to create a faint glow around his whole body – the sign that he was about to dematerialize. 'I love you,' he said softly.

'I love you,' I mouthed back, still willing him to stay, but knowing he wouldn't.

The light grew brighter, more dazzling until Phoenix disappeared.

Exhaustion came over me the moment he left. I just had enough strength to drive home, park my car and head inside.

'Hannah called,' Jim reported as I passed through the kitchen. 'She said she'd texted and didn't get a reply.'

Pulling out my phone I switched it on and read her

message: WHAT'S THE STORY WITH YOU AND LUCAS?

NO STORY, I texted back.

SAW U 2 DRIVE OFF. LOOKED LIKE A STORY 2 ME! she came back.

I switched off my phone again and went wearily upstairs, flipped open my laptop, logged on. I Googled angelvoice.

Comments about Summer's concert were arriving thick and fast.

Can't wait until 2moro!

So happy but so sad – can't believe it's a whole year!

Has anybody out there got a spare ticket?

I paused on this one, disappointed to see that it was from a fan named LilyZee. I scrolled again – surely there would be a similar desperate message from JakB.

But no – Summer's 'number one fan' had gone to ground. There was no green skull icon, no last-minute effort to buy a ticket and get through the doors of the concert hall by legal means. And I found the absence more sinister than a hundred crazy messages. I was beginning to think I'd been wrong and that JakB *could* literally vanish off the face of the earth.

When finally I turned off my computer and lay on the bed, fully clothed, I couldn't stop running through different scenarios in my head. The one that cropped up most was that JakB had somehow managed to get hold of a ticket. He would be there in the morning, merging with hundreds of other Summer fans, slipping into the theatre, making his way to the front of the auditorium with a weird smile. I would be halfway through my 'Red Sky' duet with Hannah and I would look down to the front row. He would be staring up at me, and the look in his eyes would say: *I won!*

He would be right. I hadn't nailed JakB. Summer's killer would walk away a free man.

Outside my window the wind blew. Through the open drapes I saw clouds drift across the face of the moon.

Out at Foxton, Donna was taking care of Summer, who was totally shutting down, accepting an eternity of doubt.

I lay on my bed waiting for the dawn.

Light showed in the sky. I showered and changed into black denims and short leather jacket, was out of the house and waiting in the school car park before anyone else showed. If JakB did turn up, I wanted to be sure to be there.

Parker Simons and Ezra Powell were the first to arrive, pulling up by the side door of the theatre to unload some heavy techie stuff. The janitor came out of his office to unlock the door and let them in. Miss Jones drove into the car park soon after. Then the performers began to trickle in. Jordan arrived in Lucas's truck, Christian showed up soon after on his black Kawasaki. None of them except Hannah noticed me parked in the far corner.

'Darina, are you coming?' she yelled from the side door.

'Yeah. You go ahead,' I called back.

'You're sure you don't want me to wait?'

'No. I'll be there,' I promised. It was thirty minutes before the concert was due to start and fans were arriving. I was searching for an old red saloon in amongst the smart SUVs and shiny coupés.

Hannah looked unsure but decided to go on in. Meanwhile I saw a red car cruise by the main gate. My heart missed a beat. A red car, but was it JakB? Why hadn't he turned into the car park? Getting out of my car, I ran up to the street.

The red car was stationary, waiting for a light to turn green. I looked more closely – it was too new and shiny. The lights changed and the car pulled away.

It was when I made up my mind that it was time for me to go inside the building and search there that I saw him.

I was on foot, crossing the car park when a figure

stepped out from behind the row of tall redwoods planted as a wind break to shelter the main school building. My heart played up again, almost stuttering to a total halt.

'It's all good,' JakB told me in a calm voice. I was about to say *happy* voice, but the guy's emotions were too weird to fit that. He had a smile on his face, but he sounded flat and detached. 'I talked with Summer. She understands.'

'I knew she would,' I said carefully, trying not to let him circle me and back me into the trees. This was my last chance – I had to talk to him, make him confess. At the same time I was scared out of my head.

'She told me she didn't care about the concert. She's not into big gestures of appreciation.'

'Right,' I agreed. 'She's a private person. What matters is staying close to those few people who mean a lot to her.'

'You can't break the bond we have together – she told me that.'

My God – those staring eyes! I was certain they were the eyes behind the aviator shades, taking aim across the mall and firing. Meanwhile, JakB had somehow managed to back me up against the rough bark of one of the redwoods and I was raising both my hands to protect myself. 'Stronger than death,' I said through dry lips. 'Totally unique.'

'Especially now,' he whispered. His face was so close to mine that his features were blurred. 'I knew from the day she died that I was the one.'

'She chose you?'

He nodded. 'Before she died I was nothing, just like a million other guys who loved her music. But I stuck with her beyond the grave, I didn't let her go. Now I'm the only one.'

'I get it. She had to die to see you were special . . .'

'What are you doing?' Hannah ran across the grounds and grabbed JakB from behind. 'You back off from Darina, you hear!'

I let out a long sigh. The guy had been lining up his toes on the edge of the cliff, about to plunge into confession. 'Hannah, it's cool . . .'

'It is so not cool!' she yelled, shoving JakB off balance. 'Darina, you're coming with me and we're going to call Security!'

As she was dragging me away, JakB regained his balance and watched us leave.

'The concert begins in ten minutes,' Hannah gasped. 'Are you in or out, Darina? Because if you're too shaken up to stand and sing in front of two thousand people, we need to tell Miss Jones right now.'

* * *

238

I joined the tribute, swept along on a wave of love and admiration for my friend, Summer Madison. Her songs helped wash away the sorrow.

'Summer's mom and dad are sitting in the front row,' Jordan whispered to me as Hannah and I stood in the wings ready to sing our 'Red Sky' duet. 'Zoey and her parents are there too.'

'You're sure you can do this?' Hannah checked with me.

I nodded and stepped out under the bright lights. They seemed to burn into my brain and anaesthetize my fears so that I focused on the music and sang as if my life and Summer's eternal future depended on it.

Shoulder to shoulder with Hannah, Jordan, Christian and the others, I stood, chin raised, gathering air into my lungs. Afterwards, we soaked up the applause, bowed and smiled, sang our encore of 'Time to Go'. When Miss Jones turned to the audience and invited Heather and Jon Madison on the stage to stand among us, our hearts swelled.

'Thank you,' Jon told us, taking Hannah and Jordan's hands and holding them tight and raising them above their heads. Heather singled me out and stood beside me until the applause finally faded. 'Thank you for being strong,' she told me.

I was sure, as I stood onstage watching the audience leave the theatre, that there was the sound of wings soaring towards the darkened roof – endless wings beating and disturbing the still air. The stage lights died. I was certain that Summer and the Beautiful Dead were present as we said goodbye.

By midday everyone had left the building and I had checked every corner where JakB might be hiding – the empty auditorium, the backstage area, the control room with its banks of sound and lighting equipment.

'Who's there?' a voice asked and someone shone a flashlight in my eyes as I stepped back out on to the darkened stage.

I put my hand up to cut out the glare. 'Is that you, Parker?'

'Darina, how come you're still here?' He lowered the beam so that a pool of yellow light shimmered around my feet. 'I'm checking the place is empty. The janitor needs to lock up.'

'OK, I'm coming.' It was past midday, we were inching closer to Summer's departure from the far side and JakB was still on the loose. 'I'm looking for someone – the guy with the skull T-shirt. I guess you haven't seen him?'

'The weirdo who beat you up?'

240

'Who told you?'

'Ezra. He said he saved your life.'

'That's Ezra – always bigging himself up. I can take care of myself, thanks.'

'Not the way he told it,' Parker insisted as we walked backstage and made our exit through the side door. 'And if you want my advice, Darina—'

'Which I don't,' I cut in. Like Ezra, Parker fitted the nerdy image and, like him, lacked a sense of what people needed from him. Plus, everything was always so serious. 'Lighten up,' I told him.

Birdlike, he pulled his chin back into his neck, creating several folds of skin. 'I'm only trying to warn you,' he complained.

'Thanks, Parker,' I told him, crossing paths with the janitor and his jangling bunch of keys.

I was almost at my car without any idea of my next move. *Maybe I'll drive out to Foxton Ridge,* I thought in desperation. Then something made me investigate the storeroom where JakB had already sprung me one big surprise.

The door was hanging open – I guess that's what attracted my attention. I walked over and took hold of the handle, thought maybe I would just push the door closed. *I need to get the janitor to lock this before he leaves,* I thought.

An obstacle on the inside of the door stopped me from clicking it shut so I slipped my fingers along the inside of the door frame and felt for a light switch. I found it and clicked it on. Light flooded the room, brought me right up against the obstacle – a suspended body in sneakers, jeans and black T-shirt swinging from a noose slung over a horizontal metal bar above my head. JakB's body swung and rotated gently, head to one side, the spinal column snapped at the neck.

JakB had hanged himself in the janitor's storeroom. He left a note, which I found folded and propped against the seat of the grass-cutter.

Not so much a note – more a picture of a heart with an arrow through and initials at either end: SM and JB. The drawing was intricate, in the style of a tattoo artist, so that the heart looked 3-D, with a velvety sheen. Underneath the drawing he had scrawled a spidery, almost illegible message, as if all his attention had gone into making the drawing and now he was out of time.

Reunited, it read. Then something that sounded biblical: *In their deaths they were not divided.*

My hand was shaking, I was ready to throw up as I backed out of the store.

The memory of JakB's dead face, mottled and

distorted, will stay with me for ever.

'Darina?' Ezra's voice was impinging through the daze. Three figures came running – Ezra, Parker and the janitor, when Phoenix and Hunter materialized and zapped me out of there, right in front of their eyes.

I felt pain all over my body, as if a heavy weight had pressed and stretched me during long hours of medieval torture. These were the symptoms of being zombie-zapped through space between Ellerton and Foxton Ridge.

We were in the barn – me and all the Beautiful Dead; Hunter, Dean, Donna, Iceman and Phoenix. Summer was sitting cross-legged in the centre of the circle and there were four hours left before she had to leave for ever.

'So, is the right guy dead?' Dean asked me. 'Did JakB shoot our girl and kill himself?'

'I guess so.' Between Dean's question and my answer there was a universe of doubt. I gazed at Summer's face, trying to work out her reaction to the latest event.

'No signed confession?' Dean checked.

I shook my head. 'But it had to be JakB. Who else is still in the picture?'

Hunter turned to Dean, who stood outside the circle. 'Are we OK with this?'

'We need more,' Dean said slowly. 'That's why you

brought Darina back here.'

I spread my palms in a gesture of despair. 'There is no more! What can I do?'

'She's right.' When Summer spoke, her voice was slight as a breeze. 'Darina can't do any more. Let it be, Hunter.'

He broke through the circle, swept her up from the ground and carried her to the foot of the loft steps, where he set her down gently against the wall then straightened the hem of her long, dark skirt so that it covered her feet. 'Is this the answer we've been looking for?' he coaxed. 'A lonely guy, a twisted fantasist who couldn't bear to live once he realized what he'd done to the girl he adored?'

'Yes – I don't know.' Summer trembled with the effort of speaking. Her eyes had sunk deep into their sockets, though her hair caught in the sunlight and shone like gold.

'You're certain that you want me to let it be?' Hunter asked.

She reached out her hand to me and I went to join her and Hunter. 'Thank you, Darina.'

I closed my eyes. Fichtner – not guilty. Thorne and Stone – not guilty. JakB – dead. But guilty or not guilty? Without a suicide note confessing what he'd done, the question was unanswered. I opened my eyes to look straight at Hunter. 'We need more,' I agreed.

And now it was Phoenix's turn to stride across the barn, raising dust motes in the rays of afternoon sunlight. 'Whatever it is, does it have to involve Darina?' he challenged Hunter, taking my hand as if to lend me some of his strength.

'It's time travel and no way can it include Summer,' the overlord pointed out. 'I've already discussed it with Darina and she understands.'

I nodded at Phoenix. 'It won't work. Summer isn't strong enough.'

'So?' As the tension rose, I felt Phoenix's hold on my hand tighten. 'Who gets to time-travel if it's not Summer?' he asked Hunter.

The all-powerful Beautiful Dead overlord drew himself up and looked coolly from Phoenix to me and back again. 'Darina was there when Summer died,' he reminded us. 'She's the one who gets to go back.'

It was me – Hunter chose me and me alone to save Summer's eternal soul. She sighed where she sat, surrounded by sunlight and dancing dust, and a slight tremor passed through her body.

'I'm ready,' I told the overlord, feeling Phoenix's grasp loosen as Hunter gave the silent order for him to stand aside.

'This doesn't include you,' Hunter told him. 'It's just me and Darina.'

I saw how hard it was for my Beautiful Dead boyfriend – being totally under an overlord's command, stripped of all power to resist. I read it in Phoenix's eyes – they opened with a flicker of stubborn resistance, then immediately closed and his expression faded to passive obedience. I re-took his hand but, for once, he refused to look me in the eye.

'It's part of the deal,' it was my turn to remind him. 'We get to be with each other, but we're not free.'

'If I could choose . . .' he whispered.

'You would never let me go alone. I know.'

Phoenix raised his gaze. He looked at me steadily, pouring his love over me as if it was a molten, metallic shield that would protect me in the task ahead.

'Thank you,' I whispered.

'Be safe,' were his last words.

'You know what you have to do?' Hunter asked.

He'd led me out of the barn, across the yard, and halfway up the hill towards the water tower. He'd zapped my mind so that I couldn't look back.

'I have to identify the killer,' I said. 'This is what all this has been about.'

'In spite of the risks and the pain. We go back to the mall, to the very spot, the exact moment when it happened. This time you make sure you get a good look at the gunman's face.'

I nodded. My mouth was dry, my throat constricted. 'I'm ready,' I said again.

'And, Darina . . .' Hunter wasn't looking at me – his gaze was directed up at the ridge, towards the aspen stand and the spring-green leaves fluttering against the blue sky.

'I respect you for this.'

Life was full of surprises, but none bigger than any compliment from the stern, stone-cold overlord. For a second I thought I hadn't heard right.

'You've grown – as a person, since you first came out here to Foxton Ridge with your breaking heart and your despair. You're working through that with courage and loyalty. Now I see strength in your actions.'

'I'd do anything for Summer,' was my explanation.

'And for Phoenix.'

'He means more than life, believe me.'

'I see he does,' Hunter murmured, reading my mind, my heart. 'After Summer, Phoenix will be next.'

I tried to swallow but couldn't. Neither could I move one step up the hill, or look anywhere except at Hunter's strong, impassive features. 'Were you always this way?' I whispered. *So stern and suspicious, so unbending.*

He ignored my question. 'You'll help Summer through these next, final hours, then you'll help him. This much I promise.'

'And will you be here?' *Or Dean, or another overlord?*

Hunter shrugged. 'That's outside my control. Time will tell. One more word, Darina – you left off your investigations into my wife's affairs, which shows you are wiser than you were when we first began.'

That's because I was too scared to go there! The corners of my mouth twitched into an almost-smile. 'You sound like my teacher in school, raising my grades from C to B.'

'Less headstrong.' He overrode my attempt to brush the praise aside and carried on digging deep below my surface. 'More generous and thoughtful. You begin to see things from another point of view.'

I smiled, and this time it was genuine. 'I'm sorry if I ever put you in danger out here. I never planned it that way.'

'Not a problem,' he acknowledged. 'I first chose you as our contact with the far side because of who you are, and that includes your rebelliousness, your impatience, your passionate nature.'

'Is that me?' I guess it was. If anyone knew me from the inside out, it had to be the master mind-reader and leader of the Beautiful Dead.

'So,' Hunter said, releasing me from his powerful gaze and striding on up the hill. 'It's time.'

We stood under the aspens. Sunlight turned the green leaves translucent, the silver trunks stood like sentinels.

Then Hunter brought down the wings from above, made them beat with a fury I'd never felt before, raising a storm, whipping spring leaves from their branches, making them whirl and twist about our heads.

The wings darkened the blue sky, closed in on us, and I felt myself writhe in terrible pain and fall to the ground as they pressed in on me, beating and beating until they forced entry into my head and my body, with Hunter standing unmoved beside me.

As I raised my arms to cover my head, I felt the stirring of my own angel wings at my shoulders. I crouched. There was a dark tunnel ahead. We were spinning and weightless like astronauts, dragged into the dark. Not like astronauts – we were divers deep in a black sea, arms flailing, flung about by the cold current, out of oxygen. We were rising to the surface too fast; our bodies couldn't take the pressure. Every muscle, every sinew was shot through with pain. We could not breathe.

And then there was a light. Hunter took my hand and pulled me towards it, his own wings beating, an iron look on his face that said he would not be beaten.

The black, whirling force of time resisted him – *Go back! Go back!* He fought on, kept hold of my hand, took me with him.

I wanted to scream – at the power of the black vortex, the agony of the journey, and now at the death heads, the skulls clattering against each other, cracking and splitting, falling away in fragments, while the dark holes of their eye sockets surrounded us. Death was there in that space, driving down on us, trying to claim us.

No breath. No air in my lungs. I was suffocating and the distant light was too far away. For an instant I knew I would die.

It wasn't so bad – after all, I wasn't afraid. Death could have me, I wouldn't fight it. Then maybe Phoenix and I would be together.

A hurricane of skulls and wings, Hunter dragging me on towards the light, the whole world spinning, me tumbling and beginning to spread my own angel wings, leaving Death behind.

A surprise – I fought against the dark at last. Together Hunter and I flew towards the light.

It grew bigger, brighter. It surrounded us and overcame the darkness. Bright white light, shining, cold. Hunter and I left the darkness behind and welcomed the stillness, the silence of that light. I thought I heard Phoenix's soft voice saying, *'You're safe, my love.'* And when I looked around again, I saw a shiny glass-and-metal escalator silently ascending into a huge atrium and beneath it, an expanse of white marble floor.

There was I, sitting reading a book in Starbucks. I wore my short plaid skirt and black, cropped jacket, my hair a little shorter than I wear it now.

Shoppers came and went across the mall floor, ascended the escalator, disappeared into the atrium.

Angel-me saw that I was restless, turning the pages of the book without really reading, looking at my watch, and angel-me remembered that I was due to meet Phoenix later that day when Summer was shot. I was killing time in Starbucks, waiting, longing to be with him.

There was hardly anyone else in the coffee shop, I noticed. A woman with a small kid – a boy maybe three years old, a man with a newspaper at the counter ordering skinny latte.

Invisible with Hunter at the base of the escalator, angel-me scanned the shops opposite Starbucks. There was a high-end shoe store, another coffee place and the music shop. Sinuous guitars gleamed in the window, automatic doors slid open and Summer walked out. 'Stop!' I wanted to yell. 'Don't move. Stay right where you are!'

She was carrying a small yellow bag containing CDs. She turned to say something to someone inside the store. Then she waved and walked towards coffee-shop-me.

Angel-me turned to Hunter. 'Please!' I begged. I don't know what I meant.

He got inside my panicking head and redirected my gaze back to Summer.

She was walking towards me in Starbucks, smiling. 'Hi, Darina!' she called. She wore a long, dark-green skirt with a sheen like a raven's wing. Her golden hair tumbled over her shoulders. My angel-pity for her overwhelmed me.

A guy came out of the music store after her. He was calling her name. Still smiling, she turned to speak with him.

The shots sounded like they were fake – a high cracking sound, not a boom. I heard three shots in quick succession, maybe four.

Summer stood until he fired the third bullet. At the fourth, she fell to her knees. She looked up towards the light shed by the glass roof of the tall atrium. The fifth shot, the fatal one, hit her in the heart.

I saw Summer's look of bewilderment, imagined but could not hear her gasp as people began to scream and run. Then she was lying on the floor in a pool of her own blood.

More screams. Coffee-shop-me sat where I was, shock delaying my gut reaction, which was to run to where Summer lay. Angel-me saw the mother grab her three-year-old and the man with the newspaper beat a retreat behind the counter. Out in the mall, the crowd split and fled, the reverse of iron filings to a magnet. The gunman

253

in the black T-shirt and white cap still aimed his gun directly at Summer.

Why was the sun shining down through the roof? Why didn't God or someone, something strike the guy dead where he stood?

I got up from my Starbucks chair and ran towards Summer. She was still alive, her breathing shallow, looking up at me with what I can only call wonderment.

'You'll be OK,' I promised, cradling her head, watching her eyelids flutter closed. I so longed for her to be, pressing my hand against her chest to stem the flow of blood because I knew that's what you had to do.

The look of wonder passed. She didn't open her eyes again.

A uniformed security guard ran the wrong way down the up-escalator. The gunman saw him and re-aimed his weapon. He missed the guard but the guy lost his balance and rolled down the moving steps, giving the killer time to choose which way to run.

'Summer, it's going to be OK,' I whispered, until Hunter bent over us, his wings spread wide like a shelter, and made me release her.

'You have to follow him!' he urged. 'Go, Darina!'

Angel-me eased Summer on to the floor, took a second to lift her hair clear of her shoulders so as not to get it bloody, and to smooth her skirt. Then I was up and running after the killer, who sprinted past the music store towards the exit, past dozens of cowering shoppers. I saw his back view – the slight frame, the dark clothes, and one time a glimpse of his thin face with the aviator shades when he glanced over his shoulder to check if he was being followed.

This time he was, though he didn't know it.

I flew after him down the marble slope, out through the main exit.

He was on the street, sprinting towards the car park next to a gas station, looking over his shoulder. I was faster, gaining on him though he couldn't see me. I could hear the soft thud of his sneakers on the sidewalk, his dry, grating breaths.

People took one look at the gun in his hand and pressed themselves to the wall, and this was when Hunter stepped in. I felt him overtake me in a rush of beating wings – they were more powerful than the killer's fastest sprint. Soon Hunter was ahead, blocking his way. He put out one hand to stop him in his tracks.

The gunman ran smack into the invisible barrier and went reeling backwards. He lost his gun as he sprawled on the ground, then rolled and tried to get up.

Hunter stood back and left the rest to me.

I grabbed the gun from the sidewalk. I stamped hard on the killer's wrist, pinned him down and heard him yelp. Then I fell to my knees and ripped off that white cap, took off the shades and flung them aside.

His hair was the colour of straw. There was a bruise-coloured birthmark under the left eye.

JakB had hung himself in the janitor's storeroom. He left a note, which I found folded neatly and propped against the seat of the grass-cutter.

Not so much a note – more a picture of a heart with an arrow through and initials at either end: SM and JB. The drawing was intricate, in the style of a tattoo artist, so that the heart looked 3-D, with a velvety sheen. Underneath the drawing he had scrawled a spidery, almost illegible message, as if all his attention had gone into making the drawing and now he was out of time. Reunited, *it read. Then something that sounded biblical:* In their deaths they were not divided.

My hand was shaking, I was ready to throw up as I backed out of the store.

The memory of JakB's dead face, mottled and distorted, will stay with me for ever.

'Darina?' Ezra's voice was growing louder. Three figures came running – Ezra, Parker and the janitor.

From outside the storeroom the janitor saw the bottom half of JakB's hanging corpse. He reached for his cell phone and called nine-one-one. Parker turned away, he bent forward and threw up on the grass. Ezra let out a gasp, like someone had punched him in the stomach.

Hunter had dragged angel-me back here from my time travel. It felt like I had a hand around my throat, choking me. I struggled for breath, my head was still in that dark tunnel, my body was still on the rack. The last thing I remembered clearly was staring down at Summer's killer's face and seeing the purple birthmark behind the aviator shades.

'We need paramedics, we need the cops,' the janitor jabbered into his phone.

Parker was still retching loudly.

The swinging rope rasped against the metal bar from which the noose was suspended. JakB's feet were splayed out like a fish tail.

As Ezra lifted his hand to tip his glasses further up the bridge of his nose, I reached out and took them clean away.

'What . . . ?' He tried to grab them back.

I hid them behind my back, twisted them and snapped them in two.

Ezra's eyes widened as they met mine. What did he see

there? Did he know right then that I knew?

'Sorry, I don't know what I was thinking,' I gasped, showing him the broken shades. Events were racing on – the paramedics and the cops were on their way, Parker had finished retching and the janitor was saying for us not to touch a thing. 'I have a spare pair of shades. They're in my bag. I left it in the theatre.'

He took his wrecked pair from me, looking like he might cry. You never saw Ezra without his shades, never saw that disfiguring mark – that Rorschach blotch that, to me, had a weird, angel-wing similarity.

'I can get them for you,' I volunteered. 'I'll show you.'

'Don't go anywhere,' the janitor warned me. 'You're the main witness.'

'I'll be five minutes,' I promised. 'Come on, Ezra.'

He followed me across the car park, in through the main door of the theatre. I reckoned correctly that, to him, covering his birthmark mattered more than anything.

We were in the empty auditorium, minus daylight, feeling our way down the broad central aisle and up the steps on to the stage. Dimly lit signs above the doors showed the side exits.

'I guess it was the shock,' I explained. 'Maybe I was trying to grab your hand for something to hold on to.'

258

'Whatever,' Ezra mumbled. He seemed calm and in his element, up on the stage with me, surrounded by snaking cables, microphones and lights. With the toe of his sneaker he clicked a switch on the floor which brought on a solitary overhead spot.

'My bag is in a locker next to the girls' dressing-room.' *Keep a grip, don't look scared.* I faked a smile – I actually managed to do that. 'Honestly, Ezra, I like you better without your glasses.'

His hand went up to the purple mark.

'You don't even notice,' I assured him. 'Believe me.'

'You say that,' he muttered. 'But people stare.'

'Not in a bad way.'

'Yes, in a bad way. Kids in kindergarten used to point or sometimes they totally freaked out.'

'Not now we're older.' Dipping into my pockets, I acted out a search for the locker key. Failing to find it, I stopped by the water fountain to fill a plastic cup. 'Everyone has something they're ashamed of. Take Logan – he hated that he had curly hair.'

Mention of Logan's name made Ezra put his hand up to cover the mark – he really couldn't stop himself.

I took a sip of water, inched forward with the pressure. *Don't freak him out, push him slowly, slowly . . .*

'And Logan hated that he was jealous.'

259

'What about?' The hand dropped from the mark. Ezra looked hungry for more.

'About everything.' I shrugged. I was doing it – putting on the act, hiding my terror. 'I'll tell you something – Logan had a huge crush on me. He was jealous of everything and everyone who came within half a mile.'

'Do you miss him?'

'Some.' *Forgive me, Logan. I hope you understand.* 'He was jealous of you, Ezra. Did you know that? Yeah, 'course you did – you two had that fight.'

We stood under the spotlight, Ezra and me. I carried on fly-fishing, casting my line to hook him.

'Logan said for me to back off,' Ezra admitted. 'He said no way would you notice me.'

'Like I said – he could get crazy with jealousy. But honestly, I never felt that way about him.'

'So he was wrong? Should I have let you know the way I felt?'

Look Ezra in the eye. Light-brown, honey-coloured eyes set shallow in their sockets with drooping upper lids, the dead-straw hair spiking straight up from his forehead, thin cheeks, a heavy underlip mis-matching the thin, wide upper one. His bottom lip was pulpy and moist.

'Yeah, 'cos what am I – a mind-reader?' I actually joked. 'But then again, I guess I picked up the signals. So there

260

was totally no need for you two guys to fight.'

'Logan acted like he was Mr Big and he made me mad.' Suddenly Ezra was feeling safer with me, walking across the stage to tidy some cable into a neat coil, then coming back under the light. 'He said I should back off, you were too good for me. Why did he need to say that?'

'Exactly. But it worked.'

'How come?'

'You did back off. In fact, I heard you called me some mean names.' Another sip of water, another step towards gaining Ezra's trust.

'Sure – that was because I didn't get you like I'd planned. But I got him.'

'You got him?' *I know, I absolutely know what you're about to tell me!*

The light was hot and intense. It narrowed the pupils in Ezra's staring eyes until they were all honey-coloured iris. 'They told me there would be payback time with Logan, even if it took a while. They said it doesn't matter how long you have to wait – there will come a time.'

His soft red lip shone with spittle; beads of sweat appeared on his forehead and cheeks. I listened without even asking what he meant by 'they'.

'They're always right. I mean – they see things from the outside, they employ a perfect rationality, which a guy like me appreciates. They figured sooner or later Logan would put himself in a position where he was vulnerable, where I wouldn't have to do hardly anything.'

I had stopped breathing. I struggled to suppress a scream rising up into my throat.

'It happened. The night of the storm out at Foxton. Logan said something else that made me mad – like, I had to quit even thinking about you, Darina.'

'Oh!' I sighed. Ezra misinterpreted it as a signal to move in close. He put his arm around my waist and stepped me back out of the circle of light like two dancers about to waltz.

'Logan had no right,' he whispered in my ear. 'That's when I made my plan to get out of that cabin and lie in wait. Sure, it was dark, but that was good. Plus the rain and the wind – all good.'

'You waited for Logan to leave the cabin?'

Ezra put his cheek against mine. He gripped me tighter around the waist so that I lost hold of the cup and water spilled down the front of Ezra's T-shirt. 'It was more than luck that he came out and drove off in his car – it was meant to be.'

'They told you that?' He stepped me across the stage in the dance-hold, breathed me in, swung me round.

'Fate, they said. I followed him as far as the track went.

Logan didn't even see me, something crazy was happening to him out there in that storm.'

He was taking care of me. He gave his life. My legs went weak. I relied on Ezra to hold me up.

'All good, all good,' he chanted, his lips on my cheek. 'Wind and rain. No moon or stars. Christ knows what he was searching for.'

Me! Me!

'So easy,' Ezra breathed, relaxing his hold. 'Logan reached a ledge, the edge of the world. "Push!" they told me. And I did.'

I needed to sit down. My legs collapsed under me and I dropped to the floor. I was in an empty theatre with a double killer. The guy followed voices inside his head.

'It's OK, Darina,' Ezra soothed. He sat beside me, knees crooked under his chin. 'This doesn't need to go any further, it stays between you and me.'

'I hear you, Ezra.'

'I mean, I shouldn't even have told you. I may get into trouble for that.'

'I hope not.'

'I'll tell them you're to blame. You made me talk. That's what you do.'

'What do I do?'

'You look at me a certain way. All girls do that.'

'But it's a secret. I won't tell anyone.'

'Because you love me?'

The stage tilted, the whole place shook – we were on a geological fault line, an emotional earthquake was taking place inside me. 'Because I love you,' I confirmed with what felt like the last breath in my body as the familiar framework of my inner world collapsed.

Ezra sprang on to his haunches and spun me round to face him. 'Say that again.'

My voice was lost in the after-shock. I shook my head.

'You love me!' he echoed. Then he gripped both my wrists. 'But they said you didn't. Even after Logan died, they said you still couldn't love me.'

'Let me find those shades.' I made an enormous effort to speak and make him let go.

'I don't care about the shades,' he argued. 'Be quiet – they're helping me to figure something out. Yes – Darina, I think you're lying to me.'

'No, really—'

'You are. That's another thing you do. I'm learning all the time about how you use guys. You never say what you truly mean.' His face changed, setting into firmer lines. The fleshy lids almost closed.

I pulled away from him, but he was too strong. Instead of letting me break free, he stood up and dragged me after him, towards the small booth at the side of the stage which housed the lighting board and the sound system. He leaned on the glass door and we half fell inside. The door swung shut after us.

'We need to go back,' I gasped. 'The cops, the paramedics . . .'

'No. They're saying for us to stay here, not to trust you, you're the same as Summer Madison.'

I groaned from the pit of my stomach.

'Yeah,' he smiled. 'To look at Summer you'd say she was pretty near perfect. And guys were always falling in love with her, like that loser hanging at the end of the rope, for example.'

'But you're not JakB,' I argued hopelessly. 'He was totally out of control.'

'Right. His trouble was, he didn't apply logic.'

'I never saw anyone so desperate.'

'To get the backstage pass. I know. I was never like that with Summer – I always knew where my boundaries lay. When she told me to back off, I could do it, no problem. In fact, it's them I have to thank – they didn't even let me get close to sharing with her how I felt because they knew how she'd laugh in my face. They just said for me to forget her, or deal with her so she couldn't get to me any more.'

'Summer never knew how you felt?'

Ezra pushed me back against the lighting board. He

266

stood with his back to the door, not seeing the figure who had walked down through the auditorium and slowly up the steps on to the stage.

'What was the point? Was I going to join a line of a dozen other guys in school and a thousand mindless fans? They said forget Summer or deal with her.'

I recognized the figure. It was Parker, come looking for us so I could talk to the cops. *Walk this way!* I pleaded silently. *It's confession time. Listen to what your buddy has to say!*

'How?' I asked Ezra. 'How did you deal with the Summer problem?'

His eyes flashed open. 'It's OK – I won't share with her,' he promised his voices. 'I know – I already said too much.'

Parker chose the wrong direction. He walked off into the wings at the far side of the stage. I tried to draw breath.

'No problem,' Ezra muttered as if he was under fresh pressure. He sounded angry with his voices, or with me. 'I know what I'm doing.'

'OK, no more questions,' I gasped as he moved in on me. I looked for a weapon in his hand – a gun or a knife.

'Think it through with me, Darina. Is there any clear reason why you should walk out of here?'

'Yes. You want me to love you? Give me time, Ezra.'

'You mean, don't give up on you? So where do I come in line? Is it after Logan Lavelle, after Phoenix Rohr? Are there any guys who are not dead that I should be aware of?'

'No one,' I murmured. He was standing so near I could feel the heat of his body through the damp shirt.

He raised his left hand to his birthmark. 'You made a big mistake,' he said coolly. 'You said you liked me better without my glasses. So I knew you were lying, right from the start of this conversation.'

I gave up the pretence, pushed him backwards with both hands. 'And I knew about what you did to Logan!' I cried. 'And now Summer. I know it all!'

Knocking him off balance, I reached the glass door before he hooked his arm around my neck and dragged me back, half choking me.

He kept up the pressure against my throat with the crook of his arm. I struggled, knowing that he planned to kill me with his bare hands – no gun, no high ledge to push me from. He put pressure on my throat, bending me backwards and sticking his knee in the small of my back until it felt as though he would snap my spine. My eyes rolled upwards and I could see his thin, vicious upside-down face.

I kicked. I did fight back.

And then there was a burst of white light inside the booth.

One second it was me fighting Ezra alone, the next Phoenix appeared, radiating light.

He filled the room. He blinded us with his beauty and his strength. Phoenix as I'd first seen him when he returned to the barn – stripped to the waist, broad-shouldered and narrow-hipped, pale as death.

Ezra stared at him, totally shocked. This time his voices didn't help him compute what was taking place.

Phoenix reached out and took hold of a thick cable leading to the lighting board. He wrenched it free like he was snapping sewing thread and held the raw end above his head.

Ezra saw the arc of yellow sparks crackle from the wire, knew the current should have felled Phoenix on the spot. He let go of me and got ready to burst out of the booth. I dropped to the floor.

Phoenix swung the heavy cable around his head like a lasso. It sparked and fizzed when he threw it, wrapped itself around Ezra's neck, connected with the wet shirt and let the volts shoot through him.

Ezra's head jerked back. His hand shot up to wrench himself free of the cable, but the muscles in his arm locked, the current gripped him and his heart juddered to a halt.

Phoenix turned towards me before his knees buckled and he dropped to the floor beside Ezra. He gave me the ghost of a smile.

I bent over him, begging him to open his eyes.

He lay with his head turned towards me. His light was fading, his power was draining away.

I'd seen this before – the Beautiful Dead flee from lightning storms, they can't be near electrical current of any kind. If it happens, they fade and dissolve.

They never come back.

'Why did you do that?' I sobbed, raising his head clear of the floor and stroking the hair back from his forehead. I kissed the smooth, pale skin, willing him to stay with me.

Beside us, Ezra sprawled face up, one arm locked crossways across his chest, the live wire still sparking through his body.

Phoenix had risked everything, and so did Hunter and Dean.

They came to us in the death booth, materializing in that suffocating space. Their light blazed as Phoenix faded.

Hunter bent over and lifted Phoenix. He stood tall,

bearing his weight without effort. I saw he was strong where Phoenix was weak.

I took Dean's hand. He made me tear my gaze away from Phoenix and fold myself into his arms, ready for the journey.

I was hurting again and the wings were beating, the light blazing all around. I had my arms locked tight around Dean's neck.

Donna held open the barn door to let us in.

Outside in the still, silent yard, a late-afternoon sun cast long shadows.

'Where's Phoenix?' Donna asked, her eyes shaded with dread.

'With Hunter.' It was time for Dean to unlock my arms and sit me down on the worn and splintered steps. He surveyed the gloomy interior of the barn. 'What about Summer?'

'Upstairs, sitting in the last rays of the sun.'

I closed my eyes and held my breath, prayed that Hunter's light would soon lift the gloom and that Phoenix would open his eyes and grow strong again.

An age passed. The door opened and Hunter walked in. Alone.

A shock went through my heart. It stopped. I wanted

it never to start again.

Hunter's frame was outlined against the daylight, his features lost in shadow.

As I tried to stand and run towards him, he raised his hand. 'There's hardly any time – only minutes,' he warned.

'What happened to Phoenix? I need to know.'

Hunter looked beyond me, up towards the top of the steps and my heart flooded with joy as I saw my Beautiful Dead saviour with his arm around Summer. She leaned against him. He was strong again.

'Thank you,' I breathed into the dark, dust-laden space.

Hunter lowered his head in acknowledgement.

Phoenix led Summer down the steps. 'Hunter and I came past your house,' he was telling her, willing her to gather her wandering thoughts. 'Your dad was in the garden. Your mom was in her studio.'

'Painting?' Summer whispered. She stumbled on the bottom step and would have sunk to the ground if Phoenix hadn't supported her.

'And playing a soundtrack.'

'Which one?'

' "Time to Go" – the song you said Darina should give her.'

Summer raised her head to look at me. She held out her hand and I took it. 'And it is,' she murmured. 'Time for me to go.'

We walked her slowly out of the barn, Phoenix and I, past the rusting truck in the yard, past the weed-strewn corral, out towards a meadow speckled with blue flowers.

'Phoenix told me about Ezra,' she sighed, and she squeezed my fingers.

I squeezed back. 'How do you feel?'

'Sad,' she breathed. 'And glad too. Thank you, Darina.'

Her face was so fine and delicate as she left us, walking alone across the meadow, glancing over her shoulder towards the barn. A breeze blew strands of golden hair across her cheeks. She smiled and turned towards the mountains.

There was a wilderness beyond, where eagles soared and snow stayed on the peaks until summer, where footsteps didn't tread. Summer walked barefoot, looking straight ahead, into the shimmering haze.

Phoenix and I stood hand in hand, at peace. He turned to me and studied my face, soaking up what he saw. 'I have to make this last,' he whispered.

'For how long?' I wanted to know.

'Until.'

'Until it's your turn.' I already knew the answer. Phoenix and the Beautiful Dead would leave now and go back to limbo. The barn and the house would sink into silence, I would miss him so much it would half kill me.

Then, when Hunter was ready, they would return.

'Stay safe,' Phoenix murmured as he brushed my cheek with the side of his thumb.

I nodded, sighed and let go of his cold hand.

In a week or two, maybe a month, he would come back to me one last time.

Turn the page for a sneak peak of

BOOK 4 – PHOENIX

BEAUTIFUL DEAD

Maybe none of it is true.

I reach the end and I wimp out – 'I woke up and it was all a dream!'

Imagine that; I made up the Beautiful Dead, the whole thing. Jonas, Arizona, Summer and Phoenix out at Foxton Ridge. I did it because I wanted them back in my life so bad.

But there really is no such being as Hunter the overlord, no zombies stepping out of limbo back to the far side – nothing except me and my crazy, grief-fuelled brain.

I play Summer Madison's song as I drive a winding road, late spring aspens rising silver and green to either side. '*I love you so, But it was time to go. You spoke my name, I never came, 'Cos it was time for me to go.*'

He's dead, I tell myself. Beautiful Phoenix, every day you break my heart. Your eyes stare into mine, but not really. You hold my hand and it's cold as death. *'You spoke my name, I never came, 'Cos it was time for me to go.'*

I drive into the mountains. The roof is down, I feel the wind in my hair.

Mid-May and the aspen leaves shake and shimmer in the breeze. Hot sun bakes my face and the sandy soil. The dirt track crunches under my tyres. I hit a sudden hollow, the Summer CD jumps and sticks – *'t-t-time for m-me to go . . .'* I press the OFF button. Where am I heading? Who do I hope to see? Half a mile from Foxton Ridge I brake suddenly. The engine stalls.

I'm half a mile from Angel Rock and the steep dip into the hidden valley, where the spring meadow surrounds the empty barn and the old ranch house. Scarlet poppies sing and zing there in the fresh green grass, a wave of wind rolls through and sighs up the dust in the deserted yard.

In the silence after the engine cuts out I'm unable to act. I sit trapped by invisible threads of memory and hope.

We never needed to talk, Phoenix and me. I would look into those grey-blue eyes and know – just know – what he was thinking. I remember the way he would push his dark hair clear of his forehead, once, twice, three times, without knowing he was doing it. And I would lift my hand to do it for him, then he would smile. That smile – raised higher on the right side, uneven, quirky. The love light in his eyes. Inside my silver memory cocoon I sit.

Should I reach out and turn on the engine? I see myself coming to the end of the track, getting out of the car, walking into the shade of the rusting water tower and pausing to gaze down at the barn.

The barn will cast a long shadow across the yard. The door will hang open. Nailed above the door will be the moose antlers. Beside it and in the old corral beyond, pure blue columbines will stand out amongst straggly thorn bushes. No footsteps will disturb decades of untrodden dirt, no movement, no sound.

I know – I've done this many times.

Once, twice, three times I walk down to the barn and peer inside. 'Be here!' I breathe.

My heart batters my rib-cage.

Four, five, six times I make out spiky farm tools stacked in a corner, horse halters hanging like nooses, an avalanche of decaying straw.

Seven, eight times I turn away. Maybe in the ranch house? 'Be here!' I cross the yard and step up on to the porch. The old boards creak, I press my face to the window pane. 'Be here!'

Nine, ten times the stove is there, the table and the rocking-chair, the plates on the rack. And undisturbed dust. I don't even try the door – I know it's bolted.

Twenty times I've gone through this ritual of hope.

Now – today – the rocking-chair will rock, today the plates will be taken down from the rack, a fire will heat the stove. Someone will come down the stairs and into the tiny kitchen – stern, serious Hunter who built this place a hundred years ago and who died here, will throw another log on the fire, he will turn to speak to someone in the shadows. A tall figure will step out. I know every inch of this person – the broad shoulders, the thick, dark hair, high forehead and lop-sided smile. Today I will whisper his name.

'Phoenix.'